MISTER
BROWN'S
BODIES

by the same author

A SCENT OF NEW-MOWN HAY
A SOUR APPLE TREE
BROKEN BOY
DEAD MAN RUNNING
THE GAUNT WOMAN
BLUE OCTAVO
COLONEL BOGUS
THE WINDS OF MIDNIGHT
A RING OF ROSES
CHILDREN OF THE NIGHT
THE FLAME AND THE WIND
THE YOUNG MAN FROM LIMA
NOTHING BUT THE NIGHT
BURY HIM DARKLY
BLOW THE HOUSE DOWN
THE HOUSEHOLD TRAITORS
FOR FEAR OF LITTLE MEN
DEVIL DADDY
DEEP AMONG THE DEAD MEN
OUR LADY OF PAIN

JOHN BLACKBURN

MISTER BROWN'S BODIES

JONATHAN CAPE
THIRTY BEDFORD SQUARE LONDON

FIRST PUBLISHED 1975
© 1975 BY JOHN BLACKBURN

JONATHAN CAPE LTD, 30 BEDFORD SQUARE, LONDON WC1

ISBN 0 224 01100 6

Mister Brown's Bodies is a sequel to
Deep Among the Dead Men

SET IN 10 PT PILGRIM 2 PTS LEADED
PRINTED IN GREAT BRITAIN BY
NORTHUMBERLAND PRESS LIMITED
GATESHEAD

MISTER
BROWN'S
BODIES

1

I'd never tasted human flesh, but I once met a chap who had and he said it was most unpalatable. Tough as an old dray-horse, salt as pork that's been too long in the brine, rank as overhung grouse. My informant was an anthropologist who'd tucked in to gain the confidence of some New Guinea headhunters and a few mouthfuls had made him violently sick. But he'd started his meal on a moderately full stomach, and my circumstances were different. I hadn't had a bite to eat for days and I was getting desperate. As our rubber dinghy drifted on through the Atlantic fog, two quotations kept recurring in my mind. *Needs must when the Devil drives* and *Thus conscience does make cowards of us all.*

My conscience rarely troubles me and nobody can call Bill Easter a coward. I've led a hard life and weathered a lot of storms with the Devil driving me most of the time. Booted out of an eminent public school at seventeen because neither the masters nor the prefects could control me, sent down from an even more eminent university at twenty, and forced to follow a variety of precarious occupations ever since; all of them tough and all of them dangerous.

Smuggler and gun-runner — oil from the Gulf to Rhodesia, aircraft from France to Israel, small arms from Libya to Northern Ireland. General dogsbody to Bruno Kremer; a big-time gangster and one of the most sinister individuals I've ever known. Bodyguard to Pedro Valdes, the dago dictator; a pleasant job though it didn't last long, because the fool got himself bumped off through no fault of mine.

My most recent assignment also concerned a dictator, as it happens: Dr Soji Asmonda, a self-styled Black Messiah and ruler of the West African state of Leonia. I wasn't employed as his bodyguard however. I had to kill him and it was a task I thoroughly enjoyed, because Asmonda was a monster. A sadistic psychopath who often tortured his political prisoners to death and gave the rest of his subjects merry hell. He also claimed to be divine; an immortal being who would never die. That claim was publicly discredited when the bomb I planted in his palace blew the bastard — or what was left of him — out of a dining-room window. A praiseworthy act which earned me the Gold Cross of Leonia 2nd class (1sts can only be awarded to heads of state) and the gratitude of the Rt Rev. Lord Bishop Gerald Hurst-Hutchins, the new vice-president, who virtually runs the country today. But, more important than praise or medals or gratitude, Asmonda's untimely end gained me a fortune: a large, sea-going motor launch named the *Mohammed Ahmed*, over a million pounds' worth of solid gold and a substantial draft in U.S. dollars.

Yes, I'd been a rich man when we sailed from Leonia and what was I now? A pauper rocking in an open rubber boat with the nearest land a good two hundred miles away. A starving pauper, and all because of one arrogant, bungling slob of a woman. I looked at Peggy Tey, lying asleep on the grating and another quotation occurred to me. *Beggars can't be choosers.*

Peggy might not be a dish to set before a king, but despite my cannibal pal's description of his feast, her massive rump made my mouth water and moral considerations were inappropriate. I hadn't asked Peg to come on board the launch, she'd foisted herself on me and she was entirely to blame for our plight. I'd been dozing in the *Ahmed*'s cabin when the visibility dropped, but did the bitch bother to call me? Not on your Nellie. 'Mummy knows best' is our Peggy's motto and she didn't even slow the engines and heave to. She kept the launch churning along through that thick, smothering fog till ... Wham! The bows crashed against a solid object — maybe a reef, or more probably a steamer whose bloody-minded skipper didn't bother to stop. But whatever we'd hit, it put paid to the *Ahmed*. The launch sank, taking my hard-earned gains with her, and Peggy and I just managed to scramble into the dinghy. I with only a pair of trunks to my name, she with a bikini and a handbag.

The dinghy had an outboard motor and a paddle, though both methods of propulsion were useless to us at the moment because we had no compass and the mist still obscured the sun. But there was also a tool kit containing a heavy spanner and a hacksaw, and I might have to make use of them unless a shoal of flying fish came flopping aboard or God laid on a miracle. Both possibilities seemed unlikely and before long I'd have to harden my heart and make do with what I'd got.

And I'd got a hell of a lot. Peggy had topped the scales at fifteen stone before the launch sank, and though she must have shed a pound or two since then, she was still a fine figure of womanhood. Hunger wasn't torturing Peggy because she had been living on her fat and constantly assured me that there was no cause for alarm or despondency. 'Do stop moaning, Bill dear.

We're on a shipping lane and some lookout is bound to sight us once the fog lifts.'

Fair enough, but the fog showed no sign of lifting and in time there'd only be my corpse for the rescuers to recover. Peg might be saved but, unlike her, I've always been sparely built and I was beginning to resemble one of those disgusting pictures of famine victims you see in the Oxfam shops.

Poor old Peggy, I thought. Though she'd shuffle off her mortal coils in a good cause and it's a beautiful thing to lay down one's life for a friend, Peg was stretched out face down, snoring away contentedly and I felt a twinge of sadness as I considered the fate in store for her. I'd enjoyed Peggy's favours on the bed — each experience had been educational, if over-athletic — and soon I might have to enjoy her on the table. A figurative expression because inflatable dinghies don't run to tables.

Alas poor Peggy Tey, though she would die peacefully and not feel a thing. When hunger became unbearable, I'd harden my heart, pick up the spanner or the paddle and deliver the same lethal crack on the base of the skull that had put paid to Ted Langdon while I was working for Bruno Kremer in London. I was charged with that murder, but the charges didn't stick. Bruno knew I'd split on him if they were proved and he bribed a prosecution witness to change his testimony. Seven thousand quid Bruno paid to set me free, but he's an autocratic swine who won't tolerate insubordination. He said I'd taken the law into my own hands once too often and we parted on unfriendly terms, though his seven thou' did the trick and the police were at a disadvantage. They couldn't find Ted Langdon's body and they never will find it. I and one of the boys slung it into a concrete-mixer and he helped to prop up a motorway flyover. He's still propping it up today.

And the crack on Peggy's skull would have to be delivered before too long. The mist and some light showers of rain had provided us with ample moisture, but lack of food had made me as weak as a kitten already while Peg was still an extremely powerful woman. If the blow merely hurt her, I might be the one to provide the feast.

Could I bring myself to do it then and there? I stared at the huge, appetizing body and tried to harden my heart. How happy I might have been if Peggy hadn't wrecked the launch. A millionaire with a private yacht, a string of race-horses, money to burn and squads of flunkies bowing and scraping at my beck and call. Dreams of a lifetime which Peg's stupidity had shattered and it was only fair that she gave me some slight redress. I reached for the paddle but suddenly realized that I couldn't kill her till hunger became intolerable. At that moment and just as suddenly, suspicion reared its ugly head and my muscles went rigid.

Peg's handbag lay beside her left buttock. A large, commodious bag as befitted its owner, and when she scrambled on to the dinghy it had been as bulbous as her anatomy. It still bulged, but not as prominently, and that could only mean one thing. Peggy had been emptying the bag, so what had it contained? You don't cash cheques or spend money when you're adrift in a small boat and I hadn't seen Peggy discard any tissues, empty suntan-lotion bottles or make-up tubes. I hadn't seen her take a damn thing out of the bag and my suspicions hardened to certainty and disgust as I picked it up, released the catch and looked at the contents. A purse and a powder-compact, a comb and a nail-file and a lipstick, a ...

We all know that most people are selfish and self-seeking, but there is a limit to human iniquity and at first I couldn't believe my eyes. Peg had a sweet tooth and a hearty appetite and she was rightly ashamed of her cravings. She'd hidden her store of goodies as a secret drinker conceals his booze, and the store had kept her in fine fettle. Whenever I was asleep, she'd dipped into her larder and then replaced the evidence so I wouldn't see it floating alongside. I examined the wrappings of a bar of chocolate and a Scrunchie-Munchie, an empty packet of nuts and raisins, a box that had once contained café cremes. The bitch had been stuffing herself while my belly rumbled and if one Mars Bar had not remained intact, I'd have brained her then and there.

I stripped the paper from that Mars Bar faster than I've ever stripped anything and the first mouthful was so delicious that I never realized Peggy had woken up and I scarcely heard her scream. 'You bastard, Bill.' The miserly porker had rolled over and seen that I'd rumbled her hoard, and she was squatting on her hunkers with the paddle in her hand and her whole torso quivering with indignation.

'You bloody, thieving bastard!' The paddle flailed out before I could defend myself and I saw stars; a cliché which I'd always imagined was fanciful, but I actually did see 'em. North Star and Dog Star and Morning Star and countless others tumbling down through the sky like silver confetti, and a few minutes later I saw the sun.

Bill Easter's god is an indulgent deity who looks after Yours Truly and my lack of faith shamed me because he's rarely let me down over the years. Since the collision I'd been praying for his help and the good fellow had turned up trumps as usual. He'd worked like the proverbial blacks are supposed to work but don't, and not one but two miracles had been performed on my behalf.

While I was unconscious the mist had started to disperse, and on the horizon and less than two miles away from us lay an extremely snazzy-looking motor yacht. Just the kind of yacht I'd hoped to buy before I lost my fortune.

The yacht was stationary, her people must have seen us, and Peg had started the outboard motor and we were phut-phut-phutting across the slight swell towards our salvation. In the distance, the rescue vessel seemed a very beautiful sight to me, and Peggy obviously felt the same. There was a smug grin on her face, showing that Mummy had been right all the time and we'd never been in any danger. She'd clearly forgiven me for raiding her treasure-trove and smiled and nodded when I picked up the remains of the Mars Bar and wolfed it. I did not smile back. My head was still throbbing painfully and it would be a long time before I forgot her hoggish greed.

Yes, from a mile or so off, that yacht looked very lovely, and my spirits soared as the dinghy skimmed over the water. But they started to sink as we drew closer and twinges of anxiety took their place. Twinges which grew into agonized stabs, because something was amiss.

Why had the ship stopped instead of sailing over to pick us up? Why was the bridge deserted and why was there no sign of life visible on the deck? Why was paint flaking from the wooden hull, with weeds and barnacles sprouting along the waterline? Why had no attempt been made to replace a plank that had been staved in on the port quarter? It seemed that we'd not only found a derelict but had also been sunk by a derelict. As the distance lessened, I saw that the damage to the hull was of recent origin and the plank must have been buckled when the *Ahmed*'s bows crashed against it.

M.Y. PANDORA... ANTWERPEN. The name and port of register on the stern were puzzling because the letters were fresh and clear in comparison to the rest of the shabby paintwork. I gave a couple of hails to see if there was anybody about and then told Peggy to circle and tie up against the rudder-post which was pitted with rust. The *Pandora* appeared to be deserted, but even a derelict was preferable to a twelve-foot rubber boat and there might be some tinned food in the galley. I could imagine several hazards in store for us, but we had to venture on board.

'Up you go, Bill.' Peggy had made fast and she pointed to the rail, but I shook my head. Courtesy costs nothing and for all I knew the yacht might be infested with starving rats.

'Ladies first, Peg, and you're in better shape than I am, so lead the way.' I grasped the post and braced myself to give her a hump-up; hump being the operative word. In my weakened condition, I almost collapsed under her weight and I was shaking like a leaf before she finally clutched the lower rung of the rail and hauled herself on deck. When I was finally free of my vast burden I stood gasping with exhaustion, and some of the myriad solutions to the mystery occupied my thoughts. Had a homicidal maniac killed a member of the crew each night and chucked himself over the side when he ran out of victims and the fun and games ended? Was there a cargo of acid on board which became unstable and fear of an explosion caused the panic-stricken rush to the boats? Had some marine predator emerged from the depths and scared away the crew? Unpleasant theories and, if anything of the kind had occurred on the *Pandora*, I just hoped that the madman really had drowned himself, the acid regained its equilibrium and the predator returned to ocean's bosom.

'Come on, Bill.' Peggy had lowered a rope ladder, I climbed painfully to join her and, on reaching the rail, I saw that no storm, shipwreck or other nautical hazard was responsible for the yacht's condition, and she was unlikely to sink under our feet in the near future. The hull was high in the water, the lifeboats lay under their davits and, apart from the buckled plank, there was no sign of damage. The *Pandora* was merely neglected and long-in-the-tooth, and the presence of the boats suggested that my *Marie Celeste* notions were unfounded and there was a less sinister explanation for the lack of life. The old tub might have been moored in an anchorage and her watchman had got bored with his duties and played truant. While he was enjoying a spell ashore, a sudden gale had torn the ship from the mooring and swept her out to sea.

A feasible solution, but not a really satisfactory one, because no broken cables were in evidence and as we approached I'd noticed that both anchors were in position. But, in any case, I was too famished to speculate and I craved for food like a drug-addict craves for a fix. Even if my early fears were correct and the crew had left in a panic, they'd hardly have taken all the stores with them and there must be some tins knocking about.

The galley was my goal and Peggy, with the same destination in mind, was already hurrying to a door in the superstructure. I followed her through it and as we moved down a dark, musty, mildewed alleyway my mouth watered and I considered a variety of dishes. Vegetable stew and tinned lambs' tongues ... vegetable stew and tinned York ham ... vegetable stew and Frankfurters ... vegetable stew and ...

Vegetable stew? I wondered why that insipid dish kept tempting me, but the penny dropped when I opened the galley door. The yacht reeked of boiling vegetables and the source of the aroma was visible — a large casserole simmering merrily away on a Calor-gas stove.

I dashed for that casserole, but I never got the lid off. The handle was as hot as Hades and at the instant I touched it, Peggy gave a squawk that would have roused the Hadean dead. Peggy didn't share my weakness. She hadn't been cracked on the head with a paddle and she wasn't faint with hunger. Peg had kept her strength by guzzling chocs and toffees and other delicacies and she had her wits about her. She'd realized that we had company and was peering through a porthole in obvious terror.

I crossed over to her, jostled her aside to get a view and it was my turn to be perturbed. Though the foredeck was partially obscured by wisps of mist, a single glance was enough to tell me that we were in trouble. I turned and bolted the galley door and then took a fire-axe from the bulkhead. A poor weapon, but the best I could think of.

A possible solution to the *Marie Celeste* business is that the ship was invaded by sea monsters who could exist without water for a limited period, and I've sometimes wondered if visitors from outer space could have been responsible for the crew's desertion. Whatever the truth of the matter, it appeared that one of those species had taken over the *Pandora*.

The forward deck was protected by a solid bulkhead instead of a rail, so that we had not noticed its occupants from the dinghy. But we'd seen them now all right and that brief glance had given me goose pimples.

A number of large, squat, brown creatures were crouched on the planks. In the drifting fog they looked slimy and fungoid and they were all peering in our direction. Each individual had a single eye. A white eye ... a staring eye ... an eye as big as a saucer.

2

Whoever, or whatever, our strange companions might be, they had not heard my hails from the dinghy, but they must have heard Peg's squawk and would certainly be on their way to investigate. Though I'd only taken a quick squint at 'em, it was clear that there were at least half a dozen of the brutes while we were only two. It was equally clear that our number might be up.

'Don't panic, Peggy.' She was still standing by the porthole, apparently paralysed with terror, and I tried to sound confident. 'We've been in tight corners before and we'll weather this storm, if you get a grip on yourself.' I felt ashamed of the stupid, hackneyed phrases, but couldn't think of anything else to say. 'You're an Englishwoman, not a dago, so show a little British spirit.'

'I'm only half English, Bill. My father was Dutch and it's you who need self-control. Just put that stupid axe back where it belongs and come over here.' At first I thought that fear had deranged Peg and then I saw that her body was relaxed and she was smiling. Still keeping a grip on the axe, I rejoined her at the porthole. The fog had thinned again and it was my turn to feel relief, though I didn't relax and I certainly did not smile. No marine predators or outer-space intelligences were on board the *Pandora*, but we could still be in trouble.

A group of human beings were kneeling on the deck and they were about the oddest crowd I've ever seen, and I've seen some oddities in my time. There were nine of the blighters, seven men and two women, though we didn't note the sexual differences then and there. Their bodies were modestly draped in long, brown, monkish habits which gave them the fungoid appearance and their heads were shaven. The sunlight glinting on the row of bald pates still made me think of enormous eyes.

'They're praying, Bill, and there's nuffin' ter worry abaht.' Relief had made Peg forget her normally genteel accent and she headed for the galley door. 'They're a group of holy men. Maybe harmless Buddhist monks on a pilgrimage and bound to be friendly, so just put away that axe like I said and we'll go and tell them we're here.'

I did replace the axe, but I selected a substitute from a rack near the stove. A little knife which I slipped into the pocket of my trunks. The Injuns might be friendlies, but I couldn't imagine any innocent reason for a bunch of monks, Buddhist or of any other creed, to be drifting around the Atlantic in a ramshackle yacht.

'Do come on, darling.' Peg had unbolted the door and she stamped her foot impatiently. 'We must go and talk to them.'

'Very well.' I followed her reluctantly along the alleyway to the deck and I approached the kneeling figures with even more reluctance. For all I knew, they might be bloodthirsty religious fanatics who'd murdered the *Pandora*'s crew in the interests of their faith and would welcome more sacrificial victims.

'Excuse me, gentlemen.' We hadn't been noticed and their faces remained bent in prayer. 'I'm sorry to disturb your devotions, but we need help, sir.' There was still no response, so I shook the nearest josser by the shoulder, wondering whether *Father*, *Padre* or *Brother* would have been a more appropriate address than plain *Sir*. However, the shake did the trick and he looked up with a startled jerk.

'What the bleedin', unprintable 'ell is goin' on?' For a holy man, the monk's manners were a bit on the rough side and his voice was a strident cockney. He pulled himself to his feet, jostling his next-door neighbours as he did so and the whole band of hope followed suit and stared at us, repeating the question and adding others. Who were we and how had we got aboard? Where was our vessel and were we alone? Where had we come from and what did we want? I told them we were poor shipwrecked mariners in need of assistance and the cockney chap became more civil.

'Assistance, eh? Yes, all mortal creatures need 'elp and there is only one true source.' He raised his face to the sky and tried to look soulful, but the act was a flop. He had a broken nose, a cauliflower ear and a razor scar ran along his left cheek. I somehow felt I'd seen him before, but couldn't think where.

'We was prayin' for guidance and 'elp when you ...' He had been about to say 'burst in on us', but *manners maketh man* was the order of the day and he paused and continued ... 'when you and your good lady arrived.' He gave Peg a gracious bow. 'You are both welcome aboard the *Pandora*, so may we know your names?'

'I can make the introductions, Tommy.' The next voice was metallic and expressionless but I felt I should recognize its owner, though his physique had changed. When I did recognize him my sense of relief vanished and I realized that Peg and I would have been better off with hostile Martians ... far better off.

'A long time no see, Billy.' The speaker was thin, his face was pale and baldness increased his sick, emaciated appearance. As he said, it was a long time since I'd seen him and on that last meeting he had been as portly as Peggy, his skin had the healthy, bronzed tan of the habitual whisky-drinker, and there was a thick crop of black hair on his ape-like head. 'I do not know the lady's name, my friends, but may I introduce Mr William Easter; an old and trusty comrade from the old days.'

Comrade! When we'd parted five years ago he'd called me an incompetent, insubordinate bastard and said that I'd better keep out of his sight in case he really lost his temper. He also said that if I crossed him again, he'd have me beaten to pulp, maimed for life, scarred so badly that no woman would look at me without shuddering, and deprived of my genitals. The last two threats seemed to cancel one another out, but that was what the sadistic toad told me he'd do and I knew that he meant it.

So, why was he speaking so civilly? Why had he been kneeling on a deck and praying to God whom he'd never believed in? Why was his head shaven and what had made him so thin? Why had he donned a drab, brown robe in place of one of his tight, gaudy suits which made him look like a performing baboon.

My acquaintance's name was Bruno Kremer and he was a bad man ... a very bad man indeed.

Holy men, my foot! — harmless Buddhist monks on a pilgrimage, like hell! I pride myself on being tough, but after Bruno had finished introducing his cronies, I knew I was out of my class. Peggy and I had fallen among thieves, but the *Pandora* was more than a thieves' kitchen. She was a floating chamber of horrors — a Noah's ark manned by animals who were as vicious as they come. They were also clever animals — the ones who'd dodged the law and got away.

Tommy Powell who led the Croydon bank-raid and killed a teller in the process — sentenced to life imprisonment in his absence.

Mavis Cato, whose blackmail activities had earned her a pot of money and caused at least three suicides — fifteen years, if she hadn't hooked it long before one of her victims plucked up courage and called in the cops.

Harry Thorpe, one of the best forgers in the business. He'd used the acid needed in that business to blind a policeman when he made his escape — twenty years.

Big Brian Mackay and his brother, Tiny Tim, both wanted for murder and armed robbery — life.

Sally Lambert, who'd fed powdered glass to her elderly lover and made off with his bearer bonds — life.

Martin Cornford, the Mayfair kidnapper. His three-year-old victim had died of exposure in a barn — also life.

Bruno Kremer himself. Even the Mafia and the Kray gang treated Bruno with respect, and if he hadn't made himself scarce he'd be serving thirty years for arson, extortion, conspiracy and causing Grievous Bodily Harm. With one exception, Peggy and I had joined up with some extremely unpleasant professional crooks and the exception was the worst of the lot.

Sir Jonathan Blake! I can still feel that soft, caressing handshake, still see those china-blue eyes twinkle and the small, girlish lips crease into a smile. Blake wasn't a professional and he hadn't killed for gain. He didn't need to because he was a wealthy man. Fun was Sir

Jonathan's motive and he'd had plenty of fun before the rozzers started to rumble it. Six children had died from the grip of those soft hands and he'd been sentenced to detention at Her Majesty's pleasure. A pleasure which Her Majesty would have enjoyed for a long time if she'd caught him.

'Poor Bill — poor Mrs Tey.' The introductions were over. Peggy and I had outlined our sad story and Bruno nodded sympathetically. 'You lost a fortune when your launch rammed this vessel, but you should thank God just the same.' He gave my shoulder an encouraging pat. A light, friendly gesture, but I was so debilitated that it almost knocked me off balance. 'Yes, thank Him for His mercy, Bill, because you are more fortunate than we are. You have your life and liberty and what are worldly goods compared to treasures in heaven?' Peg gave an irritated snort, but the question and implications were too bewildering for me to reply. Bruno Kremer might have lost weight, but he was certainly not dead and I hadn't seen any jailors knocking around the yacht. It was also ludicrous to hear one of the century's biggest racketeers talking like a wayside pulpit.

'But now to the future.' The 'dear old pals' manner faded slightly and I caught a trace of the Bruno I had known in the past; bluff, arrogant and demanding. 'I understand that after we parted company you followed the sea for a time, Bill. During that period, did you happen to study marine engineering?'

I was beginning to understand which way the wind was blowing, so I told him I was a qualified sea-going engineer and the answer was only partly a lie. I may not hold any diplomas, but I'm a dab hand with machines — any machines.

'Good, because we are all in need of assistance, Bill.'

My answer had raised a buzz of approval from Bruno's companions and he nodded. 'The yacht also suffered damage during the collision with your launch. The steering mechanism is out of action and she does not answer to the wheel. Worse still is the fact that the owner and our benefactor, Mr Brown, was knocked from the bridge ladder by the impact and is lying concussed in his cabin. That is why the *Pandora* is stationary at the moment and why your help is needed.' He looked at Tommy Powell, the forger, and the two Mackay brothers. 'If a gun or a printing press or a motor car was involved, one of us could easily repair the fault, but ships are rather beyond our scope and we're relying on your expertise.' While Bruno spoke, I recalled snatches of an earlier conversation. 'Sure, Moncelli's a hard cookie, but so are you, Billy boy, and I'm relying on you to nail him for me. Nail that wop, good and proper, son.'

'Mr Easter will do nothing till he has eaten and rested, Bruno. Can't you see that the poor man's almost dropping?' Sally Lambert had an attractive contralto voice and she was obviously an intelligent woman. Her thoughtfulness almost made me forget the powdered-glass incident and I told her I'd be glad to do all I could after I'd wined and dined and had a spot of shut-eye.

'Thank you ... or rather God bless you, Mr Easter. We were praying for His intervention when you came aboard and it is clear that He has heard us.' She beamed at me like an Israelite viewing the Promised Land for the first time. 'I'm afraid that no wine is available because we are forbidden to touch alcohol or meat, but everything else we have is at your disposal — everything, Mr Easter.'

The last words were accompanied by a come-hither look and if she'd been wearing less forbidding clothes and had some hair on her head, little Miss Lambert would have been an attractive piece. But I was too tired to feel desire and too confused to think lucidly. All we had experienced since joining the yacht was like a crazy, disjointed nightmare and nothing made sense. A bunch of completely immoral crooks, praying to God on their knees. Bruno Kremer spouting about treasure in heaven and knocking off alcohol when he used to down a bottle and a half of scotch a day. A mysterious and unconscious benefactor, called Mr Brown, who owned the *Pandora* and appeared to be the only person on board who could run her.

Mumbo-Jumbo ... Hocus-Pocus ... The Three-Card trick. Our arrival must have been noticed, an act had been laid on for our benefit and I was determined to know why. Though Peggy and I were heavily outnumbered and I was as weak as a kitten, my help was a valuable commodity and till Mr Brown recovered, I had the whip-hand and the ball was in my court. The clichés kept running through my mind as I considered the situation. Some job was in the offing; possibly piracy or smuggling, but more probably Paki-running. The *Pandora* had a fairly large displacement and a few dozen Asians could be snugly tucked away in her hold. Whatever our new-found buddies were up to, it was only fair that we were given an outline of their plans and promised a share of the profits.

'Right, Bruno,' I said and I winked at him. 'We know each other, we trust each other, so let's cut out the charades and the Holy Joe games. You're all hunted criminals on the run and you've joined forces for a criminal reason. Before I lift a spanner to that steering gear, I want to know what the scheme is and where you're heading.'

'Our destination is England, sir, and we have no criminal intention.' Sir Jonathan Blake answered me. 'We are prodigals who have strayed away too long and we are going home.'

'Home?' At first I thought I'd misheard him or he'd made a poor joke, but his eyes were quite frank and the others nodded in agreement. 'You mean you're on your way to the Old Bailey and maximum-security prisons. Or Broadmoor in your case, Sir Jonathan.' I stared at their faces in disbelief. 'Are you all crazy? Don't you realize that you're top of the pops on the wanted list and will be under lock and key as soon as you land?'

'A risk we must take, Bill, though I don't believe it is a serious one.' Bruno spoke with complete conviction. 'You are an old friend, but you failed to recognize me at first and the police have lost interest in us long ago. I think Mrs Tey is beginning to remember why.'

'No — no — don't come near me. Keep 'em away from me, Bill.' Bruno had taken a step forward and Peggy drew back in panic, clutching my hand for protection. 'What he says is true. All of it's true and I read about them in the papers before we left for Leonia.' Her teeth were chattering and her face reminded me of one of those Greek theatrical masks portraying terror.

'They're not crazy, Bill. They're dead ... dead bodies ... dead and buried.'

3

Legally, Peggy was right and our shipmates were corpses. Certificates signed by a prison governor, a medical officer and the lieutenant in command of a firing-squad testified to that, and a British consul had viewed their mass grave and departed satisfied. Where officialdom was concerned, they were as dead as old Marley and the doornail. The only snag was that they'd been resurrected.

Bruno and Sally Lambert were the main story-tellers and we listened to them while tucking into the vegetable stew. Not an exciting meal, but a nourishing one and just what was needed, because meat would have done my rumbling stomach no good at all. I was also glad that it didn't excite me because I wanted to pay attention to the tale and understand what Peggy and I were up against.

South America is still the main haven for fugitives from justice, but the emergent African nations take a fair share and till recently Leonia had had no extradition treaty with Britain. What it did have was President Soji Asmonda, who turned a tolerant eye on foreign visitors — provided those visitors were persons of substance with the financial means to bolster his flagging economy. News soon spread that Leonia was the best funk-hole of the lot and numbers of wanted felons sought sanctuary in the shadow of Asmonda's wing.

An accommodating wing. No long and tiresome interrogations bothered them on arrival and the only moot question was, 'How much money are you bringing into the country, sah?' Provided the answer was satisfactory, a red carpet was laid out and the life of Reilly began.

The expatriates found their new home a paradise from the word go. Land was cheap. Comfortable, air-conditioned bungalows, each with its private beach, could be constructed at moderate cost and grinning Uncle Toms and Aunt Chloes queued up for the privilege of doing the chores and bringing in the *sundowners*. The Leonese appeared to be the most civil people in the world and black really did seem beautiful. I gathered that even Sir Jonathan Blake managed to enjoy himself to the full. Leonia has a serious population problem and the loss of an odd piccaninny or two was nothing to cry over.

Shortly before their misfortunes began, the British contingent of exiles numbered over thirty and they formed a thriving little community. Their fingers were in several local business ventures and because they were a community they felt they should have a community centre. A pleasant social club with a swimming pool and tennis courts and a nine-hole golf course. Also interior facilities; a bar and a restaurant, a dance floor and a gaming room.

Labour and building materials were easy to come by; the club house and the swimming pool were soon completed and the links and the tennis courts laid out. The opening day approached, a reception was planned and Bruno and his fellow members on the committee made the most stupid mistake of their lives. They requested President Asmonda's presence at the reception, and disaster struck.

A friendly and respectful gesture, one might imagine,

but Asmonda didn't think so. Though he claimed to be immortal, he and his Chief of Police, an ex-Nazi Sturmführer, named Gustavus von Silberwald, were terrified of assassination and how right they were. I killed them both, but the invitation was delivered some weeks before my arrival in Leonia and it cooked the exiles' goose.

Asmonda was insane and the request for his company suggested only one thing to his crazy mind. An attempt had been made to lure him into the clutches of bloodthirsty killers and bump him off in a variety of possible ways. A hail of bullets delivered by Bruno Kremer — the thuds of the Mackay brothers' bludgeons — a tasty curry prepared by Miss Lambert's fair hands with splintered bamboo shoots to give it added flavour — a squirt of acid by Harry Thorpe. The President had turned a tolerant eye on his guests from a distance but he knew all about their past activities and he never took chances where his own safety was concerned.

The reply to the invitation was a warrant and von Silberwald delivered it in person with a squad of police to carry out the arrests. The club members were driven off to a labour camp in the interior of the country and charges were trumped up against them.

A hell of a lot of charges. 'Attempting to assassinate the President of Leonia ...' 'Insulting the President of Leonia ...' 'Engaging in revolutionary activities to overthrow the government of Leonia ...' 'Plotting to enslave the freedom-loving people of Leonia ...' You name the charge — Asmonda trumped it and each one carried the sentence of death which was speedily passed. Though the evidence was clearly rigged and none of the accused was present in court, neither the press nor the British Ambassador offered any protest and good riddance to bad rubbish was the general opinion of the proceedings.

But the sentences were not speedily carried out. Black may be beautiful, but it can also be bloody brutal and quick deaths did not satisfy Dr Soji Asmonda. He wanted his prisoners to squirm and ordered the camp commandant, a boisterous character with the attractive name of Colonel M'Kimba Wilkins, to postpone the executions for a month and see how many survivors were left to face the firing-squad after that period.

Squirm they did. Thirty-one men and women entered the camp and many of them had experienced prisons before. British prisons with bunks and medical care, running water and dull but adequate grub. Also facilities to while away the idle hours — television and exercise periods, handicrafts and games and cheery chats with the chaplain. Our penal establishments are dreary places but they don't run to treadmills and whipping-posts and ball-and-chain shackles. You don't get starved or flogged or beaten up in 'em and, if you did, some zealous M.P. would have a few questions to ask the Home Secretary. Leonia didn't have any M.P.s or Home Secretary. All it had was President Asmonda and Sturmführer von Silberwald and the accounts of the exiles' sufferings probably warmed the cockles of their hearts.

Before the month was out, twenty-two of the prisoners were dead. One of disease, because the camp was infested with mosquitoes and other vermin and the only sanitary precaution was to shave the inmates' heads on arrival. Malnutrition put paid to others, and two men were clubbed to death while trying to escape, dragging their metal balls behind them.

Sport accounted for the remainder, though one shouldn't condemn the fun-loving guards hastily. Maybe between the masses of hair. 'The Officer in charge of the execution will substitute blanks for live ammunition and no one shall be hurt. Sacks of sand will then be buried in the prepared grave and death certificates signed by you and your assistants delivered to President Asmonda.

'Is that quite clear, Colonel?' Though he was looking at Wilkins, Brown's words were intended for other ears as well. 'These unfortunate exiles belong to me now and once the mock executions are over, I shall claim them. Before regaining consciousness, they will have been transported to safety and be in my care.' He turned away from Wilkins and smiled at his purchases. 'When you awake, you'll be in clover, my friends.'

Clover was putting it a bit strongly. They regained consciousness on the *Pandora* which was anchored in a backwater between Leonia and the neighbouring republic of Galando. But though the yacht was no cruise liner, she must have appeared heavenly after Asmonda's camp, and Brown's unfortunate exiles were duly grateful.

'There were a few native sailors, Bill, but they left shortly after we arrived and only Mr Brown remained on board with us.' I had questioned Bruno about the absence of a captain and crew, and though he sounded frank enough I somehow sensed he was lying. 'Before his concussion, we had no need for a crew because Mr Brown gave each of us a duty and showed us how we could help him run the ship to England.'

'To England?' Brown really was a tough cookie and an extremely plausible one. To risk a North-Atlantic voyage with a bunch of landlubbers showed courage and recklessness. To get those landlubbers to accompany him when they could have found sanctuary in Galando showed hypnotic powers of persuasion. 'You really mean England is your destination.'

'We have already said so, Bill.' There was a far-away look in Bruno's eyes. 'A place has been prepared for us there, you see.'

He was too modest. A large number of places had been prepared, because Her Britannic Majesty has a large number of prisons, and shaven heads and monkish habits and phoney death certificates wouldn't fool the rozzers for long. I was equally certain that Bruno must realize that, unless privation had completely deranged him, so I asked him what the place was.

'Somewhere where we shall have time to repent, Bill. A sanctuary in which we shall find peace and learn the joys of true obedience.' A second unsatisfactory answer. Bruno was red-hot on obedience where subordinates were concerned; that was why he'd booted me out of the gang. But he'd never obeyed anyone in his life, so he was either trying to con me or the poor sod had suffered serious brain damage.

'You have no need to pity us, Mr Easter.' Tiny Tim Mackay had been a heavyweight wrestler before turning to crime, and the table creaked as he leaned towards me. 'Our sufferings in the camp were merely warnings. They only lasted a few short weeks, but gave us a preview of hell's torment which endures for ever.'

I was right. They were barmy. All nine of them had been driven round the bend and that was a disturbing possibility. Maniacs — religious maniacs in particular — are notoriously unstable and can't tolerate frustration. Peggy and I had damaged the yacht and we were responsible for Mr Brown's indisposition. If I failed to fix the steering fault, if Brown died, we could be in trouble — dead trouble.

'Just who are you supposed to obey, Mr Kremer?' It was Peg's turn to ask a question. 'This fellow, Brown?'

'Only in material things, madam. Though Mr Brown is our deliverer and our host, he is just a man ... a ... human being like ... ourselves.' Bruno spoke haltingly and shook his head. Not the kind of shake to register a negative response. The sort of motion you make if a fly's buzzing around you or you've got water in the ear. 'Sally, just for a moment I thought that I heard ... something.'

'So did I, Bruno.' Though he had addressed Miss Lambert, Thorpe, the cockney forger, replied. 'A few seconds ago, I started to hear her faintly and soon ... soon ...

'Mr Easter.' Thorpe looked in my direction, but not at me and I had the uncomfortable feeling that he was watching somebody who had entered the saloon and was stationed behind my back. 'You and Mrs Tey have eaten, but you must be very tired. There are plenty of empty cabins available, so find one and rest ... rest till we call you.' His tone was preoccupied and irritable as though he had been dragged from an absorbing television programme to take an unnecessary phone call. 'Please leave us now, Mr Easter.'

He fell silent and Peg and I didn't need any more prompting. A council of war and a tour of inspection were required and we got up and made for the door without another word. Our companions were no longer aware of our presence. They had lowered their faces to the table, folded their hands together and closed their eyes. Mr Brown's exiles — seven murderers, one acid-slinger and one top-line gangster — were praying.

4

Every ship I've sailed on, and I've sailed on plenty, has had her particulars prominently displayed in a number of strategic positions. A brass plaque, usually in front of the bridge, states her maker's name and date of completion. Drawings and notes in the chart-room, radio-shack and elsewhere give the tonnage, horse-power, international call sign and Lloyds registration number. Certificates of seaworthiness must also be on view.

The *Pandora*'s documents were there. They showed that she had been built on the Tyne twelve years ago, displaced 620 tons and had twin diesel engines developing 700 B.H.P. But no brass plaque was visible and there was something fishy about those certificates. Quite apart from its occupants, there was something fishy about the whole vessel.

The prayer meeting had looked as though it would continue for quite a while and, after finding a vacant two-berth cabin, Peggy and I started our inspection. Apart from the door to the owner's quarters which was locked — presumably with Mr Brown lying unconscious behind it — the yacht was open house to us and we visited the bridge and the radio-room and squinted down at the hold and the engines. All was not well on M.Y. *Pandora*. Even if she'd been spick-and-span and manned by a cigar-smoking millionaire and a conventional crew of Geordies, Greeks or Squareheads, our suspicions would have been aroused and my notion about Paki-running could be justified. No brown faces peered up at us from the hold, but its walls were lined with bench-like bunks that could accommodate a profitable cargo.

The yacht was filthy in most places, which was not surprising. She'd been lying in a tropical backwater when Bruno and the others joined her, and the paint and woodwork were mildewed and cockroaches swarmed everywhere. But we had anticipated the grime and it was the lack of it in other places that interested us. Like the name on her stern and bows, the *Pandora*'s certificates were fresh and clean and looked as though they'd been recently printed, which was probably the case. If so, the ship had been stolen, the owner had reported his loss and Mr Brown was attempting to deceive any authorities who came his way with false papers.

'I'm scared, Bill. More scared than I've ever been in my whole life.' We had returned to the cabin and Peggy sighed miserably. 'I'm used to crooks — my ex-husband was a crook, but these people are barmy. Homicidal maniacs, and I don't trust them an inch.'

Peggy was too suspicious and I did trust our new-found friends. I trusted 'em to slit my throat if I failed to make the yacht answer to the helm. I trusted them to sling us overboard when the White Cliffs of Dover hove into sight and our usefulness ended. And even if they didn't — even if the Holy-Joe, Love-Thy-Neighbour, Treasures-in-Heaven act was genuine and lasted till journey's end, my future was not exactly rosy. There'd be no 'Bluebirds over the White Cliffs of Dover' for Mr William Easter. Mr Easter would either be in chokey for assisting a group of highly dangerous criminals or signing up for a job on the dole. Neither prospect pleased me, because I value my liberty and I'm not cut out for honest toil. Something had to be done to save my skin and secure my future.

'They'll go berserk and kill us, Bill, I'm sure of that. Maybe not you, because you're a seaman and they need you to fix the steering and navigate the ship till that Mr Brown's on his feet.' Peg was crouched on a bunk with tears dribbling down her cheeks. 'But they don't need me. I'm no use to them and if Brown goes and dies before we reach England, they'll take it out on me.'

'Very possibly, my dear.' I glanced at a newspaper lying on the opposite bunk. An old copy of the *Galandian Echo* with headlines stating that the world's Christian churches intended to make an all-out effort for world peace and an ecumenical council would assemble in London in the near future. Information which did not inspire me as I knew that the conference was certain to flop. World peace is a pipe dream, because our species would be more aptly named *Homo Ferox* than *Sapiens*, and unless they are suffering personally most people enjoy wars.

The hell with ecumenical conferences, I thought, and then my eyes fell on another news item tucked away in the corner of the page and an idea started to form in my brain. 'Owing to declining health the President of Leonia, Field-Marshal Joshua Hawkins, has resigned office and Bishop Gerald Hurst-Hutchins named head of state.'

A minor item but it interested me all right, though I don't like Gerry Hurst-Hutchins and I never shall. He's a fat conniver who'd pull out his mother's teeth if he wanted to hang 'em on a watch chain and he was probably the cause of old Hawkins's declining health. All the same, I'd done Pal Gerry a great service recently. If I hadn't bumped off Asmonda, he'd still be a two-bit parish priest and he might believe that one good turn deserves another. I'd been a rich man till a few days ago and, if I played my cards skilfully, I might manage to pick up a nice nest egg.

Apart from the steering defect and the buckled plank, the *Pandora* seemed to be in fair structural order and there was nothing that a general overhaul and a bit of spit and polish couldn't remedy. The yacht was a valuable piece of property, and she was probably stolen property. Her freshly painted name and crisp certificates suggested that Mr Brown, or some third person, had deprived the rightful owners of their vessel and Interpol had been alerted. I intended to do a bit of depriving on my own account and with Gerry Hurst-Hutchins's backing, the yacht could be transferred to the Leonian flag and re-registered in my name. Bruno and Mr Brown and all the rest of 'em could go and take a running jump at themselves, because Constitution, the capital of Leonia, was a mere two hundred miles away and all I had to do was get there.

'Listen carefully, Peg,' I said, lowering my voice because the prayers were over and we could hear people moving about outside the cabin. 'We're not going to England. I'm taking this ship to Constitution and provided Hurst-Hutchins does the decent thing, we'll be in the money again.'

The decent thing! My hopes faded because they were based on something which did not exist. There wasn't a scrap of decency in the bishop's huge, sagging body and he'd merely impound the yacht and send us off without a word of thanks. All the same, if we were shipped back to England, home and beauty, as Distressed British Subjects we'd be far safer than on the *Pandora* and I continued to outline the scheme.

'These nuts need my help because none of them are seamen or engineers and they'll have to swallow what

I say. After fixing the steering, which shouldn't be too difficult, I'll tell them that the repair is only temporary and a dockyard inspection is essential before we head north and meet rough weather.' I handed Peggy the newspaper. 'They'll put into Constitution all right because they've nothing to fear in Leonia. Asmonda arrested them for plotting against him, and Hurst-Hutchins won't condemn anybody for that.'

'Good, Bill, very good.' Peg's tears had stopped, because she was a warm admirer of Hurst-Hutchins, and both my scheme and the news of his elevation to president cheered her. 'And you needn't worry about the bishop doing the decent thing. Gerald Hurst-Hutchins is the soul of honour and he'll either buy the yacht from us or arrange for it to be auctioned.

'There is one snag, though.' She laid aside the paper and frowned. 'The bishop has great respect for law and order and he stated that publicly on the radio. "International law is the guardian of freedom and human dignity," were the exact words.' She quoted the pompous phrase with feeling. 'These people must know his views and realize that he'd hand them straight over to the British Embassy.' Peggy paused in thought and I saw that she was right. The only laws Gerald Hurst-Hutchins respected were those he made himself, but Leonia needed economic support and was bound to have signed extradition treaties with the Western powers.

'No, Bill, they'll never go to Constitution whatever you tell 'em. They're religious maniacs and they'll rely on God to protect them from storms and take a chance on the weather.' She spoke so slowly and thoughtfully that I could almost hear her brain creaking. 'You're a clever bastard, darling, but I've got a much better idea, so listen to me for a change.'

If I was clever, Peggy was as cunning as a serpent, and before she'd finished explaining her scheme, I knew it was far superior to mine. Our hosts might not wish to visit Leonia again, but they'd go there whether they liked it or not. The course for England was almost due north, and Constitution lay to the north-north-east. Compasses can be made to give false readings, and though Mr Brown's unfortunate exiles might know the positions of the sun they were unlikely to understand astral navigation. Provided the *Pandora* only travelled by night the deception was simple. I would botch up the steering mechanism, see that it broke down when the need arose, and I was damn sure that no one could plot our position with a chronometer and sextant.

Peggy made everything sound as easy as stealing sweets from a blind and crippled child. During the hours of darkness, the yacht would churn proudly on towards the African coast, but just before dawn broke the steering would fail again and she'd swing in circles till the propellers were stopped. The fresh repair would occupy a full day, but at sunset I'd state that all was well and the voyage could proceed.

It was unlikely that I'd be suspected of sabotage, because Bruno or one of his mates would be at the wheel when the mishaps occurred. They might not be navigators, but any fool can steer a ship through a calm sea after a little practice.

I looked at Peg admiringly and did some mental arithmetic. Though the *Pandora*'s bottom was foul with weed, she had the slim lines of a destroyer and powerful engines which should give her a comfortable cruising speed of over twelve knots. As long as the weather held fair and Mr Brown didn't leave his sick bed and rumble me, we'd be inside Leonian waters before the end of the second night with a welcoming committee to greet us. A radio message to Superintendent Abdul Hakim, Constitution's Chief of Police, should ensure that. Hakim was a credulous party and my message would inform him that the yacht was manned by a group of desperate counter-revolutionaries bent on overthrowing the new government. That would put Hakim on his mettle and he'd have a patrol boat awaiting the *Pandora*'s arrival. Before our friends knew what was happening, a swarm of mud-coloured matelots would come clambering aboard and the mission be completed.

'It'll work, Bill. It's bound to work and I know that Gerald Hurst-Hutchins will prove himself the dear, kind friend he's always been.' Peggy nodded vigorously. 'We'll be safe and in the chips again, so give me a kiss to show that there's no hard feelings about what happened on the dinghy. All's forgiven, eh, darling?'

'No hard feelings at all, Peg.' I was so delighted by the plan that I could have forgiven her anything and Peggy's not a bad old stick at heart. Though stick's no way to describe a hulking porker who can gorge herself with chocs while a partner starves.

'Everything's forgotten, love,' I said, and in my mind's eye, the business was as good as over and I almost started to share her childish faith in Hurst-Hutchins's better nature. I pictured our entry into Constitution Bay, I felt the President's warm, welcoming handshake, I saw the *Pandora* resplendent in gleaming paint and brasswork, and scores of eager buyers queuing up to bid for her. My elation was overwhelming, fatigue and anxiety vanished and I sat down and joined Peggy on the bunk.

Our tumble was most enjoyable.

5

The slumbers which followed our romp did not last long. About an hour later there was a brisk rap on the door, and after allowing us a moment to make ourselves decent, Mavis Cato and Sally Lambert appeared bearing mugs of tea and a plate of toast. Just tea, just toast — no milk or butter. Vegetarianism went the whole hog and any animal products were *verboten*. All the same, we were glad of the snack and grateful to the ladies for the clothes they'd rustled up for us: boots and overalls and a couple of anoraks in case the weather got chilly. My boiler-suit fitted me a treat, but Peg's was too tight and made her look like a fat female-impersonator in a third-rate drag show. We put them on and went out to start work.

While the ship was under way the *Pandora*'s steering pump was powered by the main engines, but an auxiliary motor could be used when those were idle. Though I had no plans to consult and the system appeared slightly unconventional, I could guess the general layout. The pump action was controlled by the steering wheel which fed the fluid aft to the servo-cylinder and the hydraulic rams that moved the rudder. After a brief inspection, I told Bruno to start up the auxiliary.

The engine fired at once, the pump pounded away, but the rudder did not respond to the helm and I soon saw why. The reservoir was dry and that indicated a break in the fuel lines. After the engine was stopped, a few questions confirmed my diagnosis.

Brian Mackay had been at the wheel when the collision occurred and, like Mr Brown, he had taken a header and fallen on to the deck with his hand still clutching one of the spokes. If the relief valve to the reservoir had been jammed, the sudden pressure produced by swinging the wheel hard over could easily have burst a joint or opened a length of piping.

The valve was jammed. At some period during the *Pandora*'s sojourn in her tropical anchorage the reservoir must have been left open, and dirt and corrosion had seized it solid. Everything was becoming clear, but I didn't free the valve and I kept the knowledge to myself. That duff valve was a trump card and would prove very useful in the near future.

It was more likely a union had failed than a pipe, and the joints in the engine-room and the wheelhouse were all sound. The fault was almost certainly at the stern, but I didn't let on about that either. I suggested that two working parties should be formed; one to replace the broken hull planking and the other to expose the steering lines, starting from the engine-room and moving aft. Bruno soon got things organized down below and Peg volunteered to supervise the hull repair. I said I'd check the wheel mechanism while they were busy and prayed that they'd be busy for quite a while. I'd been provided with a tool-box and only a little spanner-work was necessary to insure that a second breakdown would take place when I wanted it to. I slackened off a couple of connections to the activating plungers and that was that. Another violent jerk on the wheel would cause more trouble and I'd state that the whole system must be overhauled before we proceeded further. An operation which would take time — a full day's time.

So far, so good. I listened to the sounds of activity from the other toilers and made for the radio-room which adjoined the wheelhouse. The transmitter tempted me for a moment, because it would have been nice to call up Constitution and put Superintendent Hakim on his mettle, but the warning could wait. I had more pressing business to attend to and the ship's compass would have to give a false reading.

There was a pair of spare headphones in a locker beside the receiver and it only took a few seconds to remove one of their magnets, replace the ear-cap and have a squint through the porthole before returning to the wheelhouse. Work on the hull was proceeding steadily and the splintered plank had been prised off. But no cries of triumph from below signified that the steering fault had been detected and there wouldn't be any triumph till they reached the stern.

It's simple enough to mess up a compass. A disgruntled character in one of Joe Conrad's stories did it by stuffing his jacket pockets with bits of metal to create a magnetic field. A simple ruse and a suitable jacket was available; an old blue garment hanging from a hook on the port bulkhead. But in this instance, the messing-up had to be just right and a more sophisticated method was needed. The compass card had to register due north when the ship's actual course was exactly north-east-by-east; no more and no less. Bruno and the other exiles might have lost their reason, but they hadn't lost their sight. Any major deviation would be noticed and my goose cooked.

I took a squint at the brass compass-housing and grinned. A flange ran round its interior and the surface was dark with verdigris. The flange could provide a support for my little magnet, which would blend in with its surroundings and be almost undetectable, so, I laid it in front of the needle tip and slid my hand sideways. The needle followed obediently and, after I stopped, the compass card registered a five-degree error, which was just what the doctor ordered. When the voyage commenced and the helmsman set course for England, the yacht would head straight for Constitution; capital and chief port of the Independent Sovereign State of Leonia.

Independent, my foot! Sovereign, my eye! I grinned a second time. The dump belonged to our buddy, the Rt Rev. Lord Bishop Gerald Hurst-Hutchins, whom God preserve. At least I hoped he'd prove a buddy and I hoped God would preserve him till he'd helped us flog the *Pandora* and make off with the proceeds. After that, I didn't care what happened to the blighter. The magnet was obviously powerful enough for the job, but if it was too powerful and held the needle rigid, suspicions would also be aroused, so I gave the compass-housing a sharp kick. The card swung from port to starboard, returned to its phoney reading, and all was well. I felt so pleased with myself that I almost forgot that the flange sloped and brass is not subject to magnetism.

Fortunately, the tool-kit contained a tube of quick-setting resin to fix the magnet in position if I wasn't disturbed. But 'quick-setting' is a relative term, and the stuff needed seven minutes to harden. At any moment the steering fault might be located and my expert guidance required. Should that happen, I'd have to pocket both my pride and the magnet and have another go when the opportunity arose. I smeared a film of resin on to both surfaces, pressed the magnet home and waited.

Seven minutes can be a hell of a long time and those

minutes seemed endless. I watched flying fish skimming across the water, and cursed the bastards for not landing on the dinghy when they were needed. I watched the crawling hands of the wheelhouse clock and cursed their slowness. Above all, I cursed the footsteps, tripping up the companionway towards me.

'Can I help you, Mr Easter?' Sally Lambert had appeared, looking slightly flushed by her climb. 'We've uncovered most of the pipes now, but there's only room for two people to work at a time and Bruno said I was in the way down there.' I must have appeared an incongruous figure with my finger stuck inside the compass-housing, but she didn't seem at all suspicious. 'Isn't there anything I can do for you?'

'Indeed there is, Miss Lambert.' There were still three minutes left and I had to get rid of her before she asked me what I was up to. 'Another cup of tea would be most welcome.'

'Of course, Mr Easter, but may I talk to you for a moment first?' She paused before continuing. 'Bruno Kremer told us that you are the sort of monster we once were and I want to know if it's true. Are you a murderer? Would you betray your best friend for a five-pound note?'

Damn Bruno's cheek, I thought. I've never betrayed a best friend — I've never had a best friend to betray, but I was going to enjoy betraying Bruno bloody Kremer. If all went well, Bruno would soon be winging back to dear old Blighty with a pair of handcuffs around his skinny wrists. I'd also be glad to sell Sally Lambert down the river. I remembered her case and the chap she poisoned seemed a decent old buffer. A hard-riding master of foxhounds whose only fault was to change his horse for a female cobra.

47

'If I'm a monster, Miss Lambert, what the hell do you think you are,' I said. 'Cinderella — Little Bo-Peep — Florence Nightingale?'

'Also a monster, but a monster that has been tamed, or so we thought and prayed.' She broke off again and stared at the jacket on the hook with the same soulful expression Harry Thorpe had tried to produce. In Thorpe's case, the act had failed, but hers came off. For all her lack of hair she was an extremely beautiful woman and if it hadn't been for the powdered-glass incident and my tumble with Peggy, I might have warmed towards her.

'Yes, we should have been tamed and our spirits remained broken, Bill.' My first name is nothing to write home about, but it sounded romantic on her lips. Lips that had probably smiled while an old man clutched his stomach and vomited blood.

'What tamed you?' Only a minute's pressure on the magnet was required and I wanted to keep her thinking about herself instead of me. 'Your experiences in that camp?'

'No, though the camp was horrible it only gave us a foretaste of what may come.' Her eyes were still fixed on the jacket and they were terrified. 'What *will* come if I disobey the voices again, Bill? If I sin a third time and revert to an animal?' Her hands reached out and fondled the sleeve of the jacket.

'Eternal damnation — that is what the voice has promised us, so help me, Bill. Until Mr Brown is better, there is no one else we can turn to, you see.' She was still stroking the jacket and I stepped back from the compass because the resin had set.

'Deliver us from evil, Bill, and help me to pay for what we did to poor little David.'

6

I didn't get to hear who poor little David was, or what had been done to him, because a hail interrupted our conversation. The steering fault had been located and, as I'd guessed, it was a joint between the servo-cylinder and one of the rudder rams. Fitting a new union was an easy matter but clearing the air-locks and testing the system took time as did the repair to the hull. Dusk had fallen before I finally said I was satisfied, and the voyage began.

A fine, clear night for the tropics. The stars of the two hemispheres were merged in the cloudless sky and phosphorescence glittered in the *Pandora*'s bow wave as she ploughed on towards Constitution at almost seventeen knots. A better speed than I'd imagined possible and it occurred to me that a few alterations could turn the yacht into an excellent coastal-patrol vessel. The Leonian Navy had lost a frigate during the civil war — as it happened, I'd sunk her, and if Peg's estimate of Hurst-Hutchins's character was right, he might purchase the *Pandora* as a replacement.

Seven bells in the first morning watch and, unless my luck changed, the future seemed rosy. On the pretence that we needed a weather forecast I'd visited the radio-room again and sent off a message to Hakim's headquarters. The conscientious fellow would know our estimated time of arrival by now and be waiting to pounce.

Peggy and I had turned in for a bit once the ship was under way, but I couldn't sleep and around midnight I'd left her and gone up to the bridge. Sir Jonathan Blake had just relieved Bruno at the wheel, Tommy Powell was acting as lookout and the Mackay brothers were tending the engines. None of them suspected a thing. Blake's eyes were riveted on the compass card and, though lunacy is said to be governed by the moon, astral navigation was not one of his attainments and he didn't bother to look at the sky. Lucky for me — a professional squint at Orion would have sent the fat into the fire.

Yes, my luck appeared to be set fair and I'd received news of the elusive Mr Brown, who had regained consciousness and been able to take a little light nourishment. His life was no longer in danger, but it would be a day or two before he was out and about again and that was just how I wanted it. Brown's protégés were easy to fool on nautical matters, but he himself would be a different kettle of fish.

Eternal damnation. I remembered Sally Lambert's words and what Peggy had discovered by pumping Mavis Cato. The Misses Lambert and Cato were frightened all right; they all were and the things that frightened them were voices. Old, cracked voices, like a worn gramophone record, that scared the living daylights out of 'em with reminders of past crimes and their sufferings in the labour camp. According to the voices, those crimes had to be paid for or the sufferings would be repeated endlessly, and part of the payment was the monk-like dress, the shaven heads and the pious gibberish. Though I'm not a psychologist, I was pretty certain a spot of brainwashing had taken place in the camp and I strolled over to Blake.

'David? There is nobody of that name with us, Mr Easter.' Sir Jonathan's answer was probably true, but I was certain somebody called David was with them in the past and Blake's eyes betrayed him. They flicked away from the compass to the hook on the bulkhead. An empty hook now, and the jacket had been removed.

'Again the answer is negative.' I had asked another question and his gaze returned to the compass. 'To the best of my knowledge, we received no drugs before Mr Brown arrived and sedated us for the mock executions.' Blake shook his head emphatically. 'The commandant had no drugs to waste on animals awaiting execution and all we received was animal brutality. I am not complaining of that brutality — the beatings, the neglect and the humiliations. They were all well-deserved punishments and necessary lessons, but shall I describe some of the things which were done to us?'

He proceeded to do so in harrowing detail, but I barely listened. No mere penny had dropped in my mind, an enormous girder had crashed from a high building, and when he'd finished I had more questions to ask.

'Sir Jonathan, can you remember exactly when Mr Brown arranged for your release and when you recovered consciousness on the yacht?'

A three-day period of coma from the 27th to the 29th of last month. A long time for them to be under sedation and the answer seemed to confirm my theory. There was a probable cause of the divine voices, the threats of punishment and the demands for obedience.

I don't know whether a person can be brainwashed without realizing it, but I know a great deal about the late and unlamented Soji Asmonda, Black Messiah, Lion of God and M.D. (Edinburgh). I had to learn to read his character like a book before I killed him, and it was squalid reading because Asmonda was as bent as they come. His power depended on religious mystiques to awe his people's minds and a corps of foreign mercenaries to crush their bodies when the need arose. Ex-Nazi and Japanese war-criminals, refugees from the O.A.S. and other political undesirables with fat prices on their heads, who were completely dependent on their master. Being a medical man, wasn't it possible that Asmonda might have fancied a few deranged killers to swell the ranks? Being a deity, wasn't it also likely that his killers should be religious fanatics?

Dedicated, obedient, frightened killers, but also killers who enjoyed their work. Thirty-one people had entered that camp, twenty-two had died, and the survivors were the worst of them all. The cream of the milk and the pick of the crop. Asmonda had selected the real baddies who worshipped violence and cruelty and he'd never had any intention of executing them, because nine murderous, brainwashed zombies would have been useful additions to his bodyguard. Mr Brown was Asmonda's man, and bribing the commandant with money and promises of fertility was an act put on for the prisoners' benefit. After they were drugged, earphones or loudspeakers had hammered out those threats of retribution and demands for obedience, and the threats had gone on for three days and become lodged in their unconscious minds. Memories which would continue for a long time and, though Mr Brown, the kindly saviour, delivered the orders, they'd originate from Asmonda.

Only one trivial incident deprived Dr Soji of his instruments of terror — I killed him. I blew him to smithereens on the 28th of the month and the revolution started the same day. Mr Brown had had to get out of Leonia fast and he took his drugged puppets with him, though I couldn't imagine what use he'd make of them.

But idle conjecture is a worthless indulgence. Everything would become clear in time and I realized that Brown himself was a saleable commodity. Though most of Asmonda's henchmen had been killed or rounded up by the new government, a few malcontents remained at large and would be pleased to take a pot-shot at Hurst-Hutchins if the opportunity arose. As an ex-agent of Asmonda, Mr Brown might know the malcontents' names and probable hiding-places, and I'd offer him to Gerry as a job lot to boost the price of the *Pandora*.

Yes, everything would resolve itself in time, and time was getting on. The pleasant rewards in store had made me forget to look at the wheelhouse clock and speculation must give way to action. The sky had started to lighten in the east and I took my leave of Sir Jonathan and moved off to join Powell on the flying-bridge. Dawn was breaking and our voyage had to be halted for a while.

Tommy Powell may have been a first-rate forger and a dab hand with an acid bottle, but he was no use as a lookout and I found him lolling half-asleep against the rail. He didn't notice my approach till I deliberately cannoned into him, but he soon woke up when I'd shaken his shoulder and bellowed in his ear.

'What the bleedin', unprintable 'ell is ...?' He was a man of repetitive vocabulary and used the same phrases as when I'd disturbed his meditations. 'What do yer think yer effin' up ter?'

'I'm trying to save your life, Powell — all our lives.' I

released my grip on his habit and pointed for'ard. 'Are you blind, man? Can't you see it?'

'Can't say I do.' His eyes followed my arm, but his expression was blank. 'What is there to see, for Christ's sake?'

'A mine ... a ruddy great floating mine?' It was essential that Powell shared the credit for spotting the hazard and I made my teeth chatter with imagined terror. 'It's right up in front of the bows and we'll be gonners unless you do something.'

'Ker-ist ... Jesus unprintable Ker-ist!' He invoked the Saviour a second time, but he didn't need a second warning. Suggestion is a powerful force when skilfully delivered and Powell hurled himself towards the wheelhouse like a bat out of hell. The fool firmly believed in my fictitious mine. He was certain he'd seen it bobbing on the water, huge, black and threatening, and he knocked Blake aside and swung the wheel hard over to starboard.

That was that. The relief valve was still solid, the joints I'd loosened couldn't withstand the sudden extra pressure and fountains of hydraulic fluid spurted up to the deckhead and cascaded down again. Sir Jonathan's drab habit was stained a gay shade of amber-pink and the rudder ceased to bite. Another stepping stone had been reached and Peggy and I were well on the road to Constitution and Abraham's bosom.

Abraham's bosom! In my opinion, that's one of the most disgusting terms in the Bible, but it seemed to fit the situation. The opulent, silk-draped bosom of Leonia's President and Lord Bishop. Gerald Hurst-Hutchins ... my paymaster.

7

Banana fritters for breakfast, nutburgers for lunch, boiled yams for high tea. A dull bill of fare, but I didn't complain. I was quite sure that my next meal would be bacon and eggs at the best hotel in Constitution.

I thought I knew about the brainwashing; I thought we'd got everything buttoned up; I thought that my worries were almost over. I felt confident that in a short while we'd be home and dry. How bloody wrong I was!

The steering overhaul started immediately after breakfast, and nobody doubted that there'd been a floating mine. Tommy Powell was convinced he'd seen it too, and though the war ended a long time ago, there are still a few of the things drifting around the world. Nor did anybody doubt my statement that every unit of the system must be thoroughly checked before we proceeded further and checked they were.

Peggy and I didn't do any manual work. Our roles were supervisory — she had been a sailorman's wife, though only a common-law one, and what do gangsters and forgers and murderers know about shipbuilding? We kept our minions hard at it and they didn't grumble. Their heavenly voices had ordered them to get to England in one piece and they were dead set on obeying them. They toiled away like Trojans and by late afternoon the job was virtually finished.

But I was not satisfied. The sun had to go down on

our labours and I took great pleasure in having Bruno Kremer lowered over the stern to inspect the rudder mountings. An unpleasant job and a dangerous one, because there might have been sharks in the offing. Seeing the boob splashing about at the end of a rope made me think of all the objectionable tasks I'd had to do for him in the past and I wanted to laugh aloud.

The sun was low on the horizon when Bruno was hauled back on board and we started the steering engine, but there was one more chore to be carried out. Peggy had directed that the fresh plank in the hull should be fixed with screws, and that gave me another delaying tactic. Dowels were needed — stout oak dowels. I told 'em to rig a bos'n's chair and get busy while I tuned in to the weather forecast. They responded so obediently that I did laugh as I ran up the companionway to the bridge and then I froze.

At first I imagined that the noise was an echo of my own mirth. A rich, bubbling chuckle with a boom and a grunt and a wheeze in it, but it didn't stop when I did. The sounds of merriment were coming from the wheelhouse and I had a visitor. When I peered through the open doorway I saw that my visitor had a sextant and was squinting at the ship's chronometer.

The sextant and the chronometer were invented by two eighteenth-century Englishmen, John Harrison and John Hadley — we English have invented most useful things — and they are both beneficial instruments used for plotting a ship's position.

That was what the intruder had been doing and the results of his calculations seemed to be causing his amusement. He was bent over a bench-type table with his back towards me and he continued to laugh while studying the figures he had scrawled on a sheet of paper.

A very short, tubby man; almost a dwarf, and at first I wondered if he was the poor little David Sally Lambert had mentioned. He wore striped pyjamas and, because I had become accustomed to shaven heads, I found his thick crop of black hair rather surprising. He had a hairy back too, I could see it through his jacket, and when he finally noticed me and turned round, I saw that he had a fine bushy beard. There was an old-fashioned hearing-aid stuck on one of his ears with the microphone dangling on his chest.

'Ho-ho-ho.' My presence appeared to amuse him as much as the sextant and chronometer readings, and he gave another burst of laughter. 'Mr Livingstone Easter, I presume.' As he didn't look a bit like Henry Stanley, the joke fell flat, but politeness costs nothing so I grinned obligingly.

'A pleasure to meet you, sir.' His right hand was in a sling, but he held out the left and I shook it. Its grip was quite contrary to his appearance. I'd expected a soft, flabby squeeze, but my palm felt as though it was being crushed by a machine and I winced in agony.

'Did I hurt you, Mr Easter?' My discomfort was a cause for fresh mirth and he chuckled again. 'I am so sorry, but I was once a professional pianist and sometimes forget how strong my fingers are. Also, this may have added to your discomfort.' He opened his hand wide and a little, metal object clattered on the deck. The magnet which I'd positioned against the compass.

'Yes, my friend, the game is up, but no hard feelings and I am delighted to make your acquaintance at long last. My name is Brown — John Brown — and I'm sure you're relieved to see that my body is on the road to recovery.'

I wasn't relieved, I was bitterly disappointed, so I

didn't laugh at the stupid witticism. Nor did I admit that the game was up. Mr Brown had a strong grip, but only one serviceable hand and he was much smaller than I am. He'd taken a tumble before and the mishap could be repeated. If I brained him with a spanner and slung him down the companionway, everyone would believe that the poor chap had stumbled out of his cabin half-concussed and lost his balance.

'Naughty — naughty.' He nodded at the sling and I realized that he'd not only read my thoughts. The little toad had guessed how I'd react when I knew he'd rumbled me and come prepared. The bandage supported an automatic pistol as well as his arm and the muzzle was pointing at my chest.

'Bruno Kremer has told me a great deal about your career, Mr Easter, and it's not an edifying story. The black sheep of a God-fearing, respectable family, who has become blacker and blacker over the years. An enemy of society with two parrot cries. "How much?" and "What's in it for me?"'

He was so insolent that I felt like ignoring the gun and knocking the bastard's teeth down his throat. Ill-fitting false teeth, which clicked while he talked and if he'd been christened John Brown, I was Jack Robinson. I won't try to reproduce his thick guttural accent, but it sounded like somebody telling a joke about Germans.

'However, I agree with Rudyard Kipling that "there's so much good in the worst of us", and you've proved yourself a resourceful rogue.' He grinned at the deck which was still spattered with hydraulic fluid. 'A five-degree compass error — one or two slackened union nuts, and, I presume, a faulty relief valve. All very cunning, but why are you so eager to return to Leonia?'

'Because Constitution is our nearest port and with a

crew of crazy amateurs and the ship in poor condition, a voyage to England is too risky.'

'Poppycock, my dear sir. The *Pandora* is structurally sound and even amateurs can be directed, as you yourself have proved.' He listened to the sound of dowels being hammered into the hull.

'But Bruno also told me that you went to an excellent public school, Mr Easter, and I'd like to ask about your schooldays. Was there anybody at that school who frightened you — really frightened you?'

There certainly had been. I never gave a damn about the masters or the prefects, but the gymnasium was ruled by a sadistic throw-back called Regimental-Sergeant-Major Hiscock, and God help you if you addressed him as plain Sergeant. Like Brown, Hiscock was a small man, but armed with a skipping-rope he could draw blood through three pairs of pants. It was not so much the pain that I minded as the obvious glee with which he administered it. I wasn't going to tell Brown about that though, so as the scriptures advise, *I held my peace*.

'Quite so.' In spite of my silence he had read me like a book again. 'Early memories of pain and humiliation have remained with you, Easter, and they will be revived unless you and Mrs Tey come to terms with me.' He perched his buttocks against the bench.

'You are unarmed; I have a gun and I also have nine obedient serfs who will do exactly what I tell them to. But both our bargaining positions are weak and I'm sure we can reach agreement. My arm is broken, poor David is no longer available and I need your skilled assistance to take this yacht to Europe.' He was so short that his feet barely touched the deck, but he scared me almost as much as the R.S.M.

'There was a popular song in the 'thirties which you are probably too young to know, but the refrain went, "You must say *Yes* to Mr Brown". That's all I want to hear from you at present, Easter. Just a simple affirmative and then at a later date, you and I and Mrs Tey can discuss the financial side of our agreement.'

'There is a financial side?' When I'd first heard of Brown, I imagined he was some pious do-gooder bent on freeing the enslaved and reforming the sinner. Then I'd believed him to be an ex-agent of Asmonda's, bent and crazy and desperate. Now it appeared I might be wrong on both counts and I felt more at ease with him. I was also ready to hear what he wanted because the hammering had stopped and we wouldn't be alone for long.

'Naturally, finance is involved, Easter — I happen to be a financier. I am also a firm believer that the labourer is worthy of his hire and you'll be well paid, provided you work well.' He had noted my changed attitude and lowered the automatic.

'You scratch my back and I'll scratch yours, in fact.' Though he spoke metaphorically the thought of digging my nails into that black pelt was repulsive and I winced a second time.

'Go on, my boy. Ask one of your stock questions and I'll give you an answer.' He rubbed a finger across the bridge of his nose and his eyes twinkled. A finger in the pie — a nose for a deal — an eye on the main chance. 'If you and Mrs Tey play ball with me there should be quite a tidy sum in it for the three of us.'

8

Mr Brown was still a bit weak on his pins and our financial discussion was postponed till the following morning. During the night, the *Pandora* had headed north on the course for England and he emerged at eight bells wearing a rather natty wild-silk suit and bowing and smirking at all and sundry. I told him our position and rate of progress during the night, but the suspicious little sod didn't trust me. The log had to be checked and three careful sightings taken before my word was accepted.

'Excellent, Bill, and we understand each other.' The use of my first name was accompanied by a friendly clap on the shoulder to show his good faith, but the statement was false. I didn't understand Mr Brown at all; he was still a complete mystery man, so I asked him what his game was. Not to his face, of course, because we were on the bridge and Bruno Kremer was within earshot. I whispered into Brown's hearing-aid and he gave me a conspiratorial wink and then turned to Bruno.

'Mr Easter and Mrs Tey and I have some technical matters to discuss, Kremer, so keep your eyes skinned and don't disturb us unless any problems arise, there's a good chap.'

'Of course, sir.' If Bruno had had some hair and nautical training, he'd probably have pulled a forelock and said 'Aye-Aye, Capt'n', but the 'Of course, sir' was a model of humility and my respect for Brown increased — also my curiosity.

'Do make yourselves at home.' He had led the way to his quarters and waved Peggy and me inside. The stateroom was large and comfortable, though it could have done with a bit of soap and water, and there were two doors leading off to the night-cabin and usual offices.

'Good chaps, aren't they?' There was a window looking out on to the forward deck and he beamed at Sir Jonathan Blake, Mavis Cato and the Mackays, who were taking their ease under an awning.

'Yes, we're fortunate in our minions, madam.' It was Peggy's turn to receive the flash of his dentures. 'Not a sailor amongst them, but loyal and willing to the core. A grand bunch, as I'm sure you agree, Mrs Tey ... or may I call you Margaret?'

'You can call me what you like, but I damn well don't agree.' Peggy gave one of her indignant squawks. 'A grand bunch, indeed! They're a pack of murderous lunatics, so let's get down to business. Why did you spring 'em? If I'd had my way they'd have been left to rot in Asmonda's camp.'

'I'm sure they would, dear lady.' Brown's smile faded and he sighed sanctimoniously. 'You clearly do not agree with the gospel that there is more joy in heaven for one repentant sinner than for all the ninety and nine.' The sigh had been an act and he grinned cynically.

'Neither do I, as it happens, but our fellow travellers are a loyal and obedient bunch at the moment, so let us hope that the mood lasts.' He left the window and crossed to a calendar on his desk. 'The weather forecast is favourable, though it may be rather choppy in the Bay of Biscay, and we sailed 180 miles last night. Assuming we can maintain that rate of progress, Land's End should be sighted by the 18th of the month which is well within my schedule.'

'You must be barmy.' My new-found respect for him took a sudden toss. 'I don't know what the hurry is, but we won't be anywhere near Land's End on that date. You told me to run the ship flat out during the night, but she's designed to cruise at between eleven and twelve knots. Unless we slow down, the fuel tanks will be empty before she's through the Bay and you'll have to put in to Cadiz or Lisbon for supplies.'

'Oh, no Bill, because I am a man who plans for eventualities.' He drew himself up to his full height in an effort to impress me, but the gesture failed because his full height wasn't very high. 'I have told you that I was once a professional musician and, among other things, I am also a Doctor of Medicine and a qualified ship's engineer.' His conceit was insufferable, but I had the feeling that he was probably telling the truth. 'I think ahead, Bill, and when I ... shall we say *borrowed* this vessel, I also borrowed ample surplus fuel. In the after hold there are seventy drums of top-quality diesel oil. Wouldn't you agree that that is sufficient to get us to England by the 18th?'

'Possibly.' I made a brief calculation and nodded. 'Provided the weather doesn't turn rough and no mechanical troubles occur, we should reach the Channel around that date, but it's asking a hell of a lot from the engines.'

'With you and I to tend them, Bill, the engines will not let us down and it is imperative that the schedule be observed. Our lives depend on it, in fact. I shall explain why in a moment, but first let us drink to our venture.' He opened a cupboard and produced glasses and a bottle of clear liquid.

'Only vodka, I'm afraid, because it does not smell and

our companions must believe that we live as frugally as themselves.'

Only vodka! My favourite tipple and I drank the toast enthusiastically, though I had no idea what the venture was. My good opinion of Brown was returning and I felt we were going to be pals.

'Another, my friends?' We had all emptied our glasses in a single gulp and he refilled them. 'Now, before explaining my project, I would like to give you an intelligence test. You obviously hoped to sail this ship to Africa and sell her and, though the attempt failed through my intervention, it suggests courage and high I.Q.s.' He motioned us to a settee and sat down facing us. 'May I ask a couple of questions to show how intelligent you really are?' Though Brown's manner was civil on the surface, there was a sneer behind it that I didn't care for.

'Why should I be transporting nine dangerous criminals back to their country of origin, and why should those criminals have become deranged? Meek and mild cretins who believe that any lapse of discipline will sentence them to endless damnation, and obedience will produce eternal bliss?'

'There's nothing wrong with my I.Q.' Peggy broke in before I could open my mouth. She prides herself on being bright, though basically she's as thick as teak. Her reply to his first question was a negative, but she had an answer to the second all right. A brilliant answer which I'd told her myself not so long ago. My theory that they'd been brainwashed to serve in Asmonda's bodyguard or secret police and Brown was one of Asmonda's agents.

'Congratulations, my dear.' He spoke like a headmaster complimenting Swotson minor, the prize pupil.

'You're on the right lines, though I was never an agent of Asmonda. I am my own master; a merchant who buys and sells things.' He sipped at his second drink like the wise man he was. The first glass of vodka should be knocked straight back to give one a lift and the others treated with respect.

'Tell me, Bill,' he said. 'Do you know how the Nazis used to train the dogs that guarded their concentration camps?'

I didn't know, and I still don't know for sure, but I do know how some other bastards train guard-dogs and it's a nasty operation. The animal is chained up in the sun without anything to eat or drink and it's systematically baited. Stones and prodding sticks and cat calls are usually sufficient, but whips are also employed and, after a while, the poor brute is half-mad with fear and rage and thirst. Then the handler comes on the scene, a kindly chap who drives away the tormentors and provides his canine chum with food and water and friendly words. After he leaves, the baiting is resumed till his return and the act continues for several days. At the end of the process you have a dog which is completely devoted to one man and ready to tear everyone else to shreds.

'What a knowledgeable chap you are, Bill.' I had said my piece and was duly complimented. 'That was the method Asmonda decided to employ to train his prisoners, but before the handler started work, I heard about the scheme and decided it was my Christian duty to take action. I also knew about the intended revolution and broke the news to Colonel M'Kimba Wilkins, the camp commandant. Wilkins was only too eager to get out of Leonia while the going was good and a mere £800 sufficed to purchase his charges and have them doped and delivered to the *Pandora*.' Brown broke off with a throaty chuckle. 'Eight hundred quid and a promise of fertility. The colonel is a superstitious savage and he swallowed my yarn hook, line and sinker.

'The brainwashing had been only partially completed, of course. Those men and women were cowed, but hardly filled with the spirit of brotherly love as they are today.' He emptied his glass and laid it aside. 'More indoctrination was needed to make them really tractable and I used Psysolibin K, a derivative of the Russian truth drug. Sleep treatment and a technique known as "memory revival" reformed my prodigals, and when they awoke on the yacht, their personalities had altered and they were meek and mild and tractable. Robots who hear imaginary orders which must always be obeyed. Not bad eh, Margaret? Pretty good, wouldn't you say, Bill?'

'Extremely clever, though I still don't understand your motives?' I tried to study his expression but there was too much hair screening his face. Only his eyes betrayed him, and they were hard and cunning and bright with malevolence. 'What is the point of the operation? Why go to so much trouble?'

'Because I am a merchant, Bill. One who buys cheap and sells dear.' He smiled again, his teeth glinting between the beard and the heavy moustache, but there was still no humour in the eyes and as I watched them, I had an uncomfortable feeling that I was being watched myself. Not only by Brown or Peggy, but by some third person hidden in the room or stationed at a keyhole. The sensation was so strong that I tiptoed across to the main door and pulled it open. The alleyway outside was deserted, and Brown raised his voice petulantly as I moved towards the night-cabin.

'Sit down and relax, man. You're right to be cautious, but I told Kremer not to disturb me and no one will dare to spy on us. So, let's come to the point and talk about my motives.' I had returned to the settee and he continued. 'Simple motives, because my profession is trade. A modest sum of money and some glib talk provided me with my present cargo, and I intend to dispose of it at a profit.

'A considerable profit.' He pulled a notebook out of his jacket and flicked it open. 'A conservative figure would be approximately £250,000 sterling.'

'I just don't believe you.' Mr Brown must have imagined his statement would astonish us, but Peggy was flabbergasted. 'A quarter of a million for helping a bunch of half-dotty criminals; you must be loopy yourself.

'Oh, I see.' Her ponderous mind was starting to work and she nodded. 'They didn't take all their money to Leonia. The bulk's still stashed away in England and you've made a bargain with 'em. They're paying you to get back and collect it.'

'Not a bad guess, but you're wrong, I'm afraid.' The pupil was being a little dense and the headmaster prompted her. 'Asmonda naturally confiscated all their portable assets and none of our guests had resources outside Africa. Other people have though, so try again.'

'You mean they've got friends who paid you to spring them?' She paused to consider the notion and then frowned impatiently. 'No, that's not likely. Creatures like them don't make friends and there's no honour among crooks. I know because I was tied to one for seven bloody years.' Her frown turned to an angry scowl.

'You're living in a fool's paradise, Mr Brown, or whatever your real name is, and nobody'll give you a red cent for that lot. Scotland Yard and Interpol and half the world's police forces are after them. I gather there's talk about hiding 'em away in some sort of retreat, but that won't work. They'll be in jail within a week of landing, in spite of their prayers and shaven heads and dressing-gowns.'

'A week after landing should be long enough, dear lady, and the tonsures and dressing-gowns, as you call them, are only partially intended as disguises. My passengers must believe that they are religious converts and if that belief fades ...' Mr Brown grimaced and took a notebook from his pocket. 'No, ransom money paid by friends, associates and other well-wishers does not enter into the scheme at all. The key words are *reprisal, retribution and revenge*.' The alliterations rolled grandly off his tongue.

'Let us take my penitents in order of age, Bill.' He opened the book and smiled at a reference. 'I don't have to tell you that Bruno Kremer was an extortionist who preyed on bookmakers and gaming-club proprietors. The Institute of Turf Accountants and The National Sporting League have offered £10,000 for information leading to Kremer's arrest.

'That makes a start, so let's consider Tommy Powell and the Mackays.' He turned to another page. 'Three bank-robbers, and the banks they robbed are eager to stand them up in a dock and show other villains that crime does not pay. The reward for the Mackay brothers is £8,000 a head and Powell is even more sought-after than Kremer — 15,000 is the figure, because he killed a clerk during his last raid.

'Harry Thorpe, the forger. A C.I.D. sergeant was

blinded when he escaped and the police want him very badly. Public subscriptions have boosted the official reward to £7,000.' Brown paused and studied our expressions. I tried to conceal my feelings, which were of extreme elation, because I knew what he had in mind now and the brilliance of the scheme almost stunned me.

'Martin Cornford and Sir Jonathan Blake come next and they are my most important commodities. The little boy Cornford left to die of exposure in the barn was the only son of Lord Lazenby; Chairman of Invincible Motors. His lordship lacks a forgiving nature and £100,000 will be paid to the person who puts Cornford behind bars.

'Sir Jonathan is a similar case. He always moved in the best circles and one of the children he raped and killed was a daughter of Ellen van Delf, the American textile heiress. Like Lord Lazenby, Mrs van Delf lacks the quality of mercy and she has offered another hundred thou' for Blake, though only in dollars I regret to say.

'The two women with us both preyed on wealthy men and those men had wealthy families.' Brown closed the little book with a snap. 'Provided all the promises are honoured, as I'm sure they will be, the rewards for Mavis Cato and Sally Lambert should bring the total sum to the quarter million. Asmonda selected the most vicious of his prisoners to be brainwashed as bodyguards. I realized that they were also the most saleable.'

'You cruel, callous, little bastard.' My admiration for Brown was soaring, but I registered disapproval for material reasons. A reluctant hireling usually gets the best terms and playing hard to get was the order of the day. 'I've known some dirty tricks in my time, but this beats the lot and Bruno Kremer is a friend of mine.

You surely don't think we'll go along with you?'

'I know you will, Bill, and moral attitudes do not become you because you're a poor actor.' The cabin was uncomfortably hot and Mr Brown got up and switched on an electric fan. 'Also, your accusations are unjust. I am clever, I am short in stature, but you have my word that I was born in Holy Wedlock, and why call me callous when I am merely a merchant and in this instance my merchandise happens to be human?

'Merchandise which I saved from agony, my friends.' The fan stirred his beard while he talked. 'Without my intervention, those unfortunates would have remained in the camp and, if the brainwashing had been completed before Asmonda's death, they would have joined his service. You can guess what would have happened to them after that.'

I didn't have to guess; I knew, and it wasn't a piece of knowledge to be treasured. The victorious rebels were short of ammunition but they had long memories of oppression. After the bodyguard surrendered, they were tied to trees, and women and children pelted them to death with stones. An unedifying spectacle, which I'd witnessed personally.

'Then you must agree that a life of imprisonment in England is a charitable alternative.' I had to nod, and once again Brown smiled at us. He was a great little smiler, but it was a pity his eyes didn't match up to the performance of his mouth and dentures. 'We will be rendering a public service in handing these people over to the authorities, so let's scrub the boy-scout morality act and talk turkey, as the Americans say. I need your help to get this ship to England because my fall has left me weak and my right hand is virtually useless. In return for that assistance, I am prepared to pay you

10 per cent of the gross profits. Surely these are satisfactory terms?'

'Perfectly satisfactory and it's a deal.' I would have tried to drive him up to 15 per cent, but Peg has no business sense and she stuck her oar in before I could speak. 'For £25,000, you can rely on us, Mr Brown.'

'I was sure I could, Margaret.' He bowed and held out his uninjured hand to each of us. His grip was not so painful without the magnet but still bloody hard, and I was glad to hear Peg grunt as he crushed her palm.

'Now for the practical details.' Mr Brown outlined them rapidly. He had an accommodating associate who owned a property on the Sussex coast which was equally accommodating. A secluded Victorian mansion with spacious cellars where our trade goods could be stored in secrecy and complete security. I noticed that he stressed the security as though it were a vital point. He also surprised me by saying that before heading ashore in the lifeboats, the *Pandora*'s sea-cocks must be opened to sink her in deep water.

I asked why the yacht should be scuttled when she was another valuable piece of property, but he was adamant. 'Borrowed property, Bill, and I'm afraid the owner regrets his generous loan. Unless the evidence is destroyed, we, ourselves, may have to join our friends in prison, so let me continue.'

He started to do so, but I cut him short. The *Pandora* had clearly been stolen and the owners had asked the authorities to look out for her. Provided we proceeded at a reasonable speed we might not be suspected, but overworking causes overheating in engines. Bearings melt, pistons seize up, crankshafts crack. If some profit-seeking merchant skipper, or zealous naval officer, saw us drifting helplessly on ocean's bosom, he'd hurry

71

alongside in the hope of towing charges or a pair of presentation binoculars from the life-saving societies. As Peg had rightly stated, prayer meetings and bald pates and dung-coloured robes wouldn't bear close inspection and I asked Buster Brown what the rush was in aid of. Our passengers were docile and tractable and full of the fear of the Lord. They seemed unlikely to cause trouble and there was no urgency about claiming the rewards. So why hurry ... why not cruise along at an economical speed and arrive safely at our destination?

'Because time is an essential factor, Mr Easter.' He had reverted to formality and his squarehead accent became more pronounced. 'This ship is laden with nine human time-bombs and their fuses are burning away while we talk here.' He nodded through the window at the group under the awning. They looked innocent enough, but Brown clearly didn't think so and all his cynicism had vanished. 'Mr Easter and Mrs Tey, my schedule must be kept, and if we fail to keep it we will probably all die as horribly as David Jones died.' He turned towards me and for the first time I saw a genuine emotion in his eyes — fear.

'We will die cursing the parents who gave us life.'

9

... *die cursing the parents who gave us life.* A pompous piece of phraseology which did not impress me at first, because I've done a deal of parent-cursing on and off and with good reason. My mother was a morbid neurotic who suffered from migraine and constantly accused me of breaking her heart; my father, a compulsive bully, subject to ungovernable rages and unfounded suspicions that my birth was due to an act of infidelity on the part of his spouse — how I wish it had been. I also have an objectionable sister who has trained her two brats to address me as old Uncle William on the rare occasions that we meet, and an equally objectionable brother who works for the Director of Public Prosecutions and is proud of it. Not a family to be envied.

All the same, Brown was clearly on tenterhooks, so I told him to cut out the rhetoric and put his cards on the table. Why the haste? Why were our brainwashed companions to be regarded as potential time-bombs? Who was the unfortunate Jones and how had he died?

'David Jones was a Welsh second mate who'd jumped his ship at Galando and had been drifting on the beach. He wanted a passage home, I needed professional assistance to run the *Pandora*, so we came to terms and he joined us. A small man like myself, but not a strong or intelligent one.' Brown shook his head ponderously. 'Jones was a weakling with a misplaced sense of humour and humour killed him. He never took my warnings seriously, though I delivered them often enough, just as I'm warning you now.' Peggy and I each received a long, hard stare.

'Jones thought our passengers' religious mania a huge joke, and all the time we were at anchor he laughed at their piety and clothes and manner of speaking and on the day we sailed he went too far. The fool drew a chalk crucifix on the deck and urinated over it. A simple case of suicide in my opinion.'

'What happened?' Brown had paused and Peggy prompted him. 'I didn't witness the actual incident, because I was in my quarters at the time and I don't believe I could have stopped it if I'd tried. Something snapped up here, you see.' He tapped his forehead. 'For a few seconds, piety went out of the window and they ran amok. Everybody is very contrite now, but that won't bring Davie Jones back from his locker. They threw him into the starboard propeller.

'One shouldn't play about with time-bombs, or any other lethal weapons, you know. One really shouldn't.' I quite agreed with Brown's statement and I had no intention of mocking our charges' religious beliefs. I merely wanted to sell the bastards, but I had a few more inquiries to make and I put them to him.

'Have you ever heard of a phenomenon known as the Third Ear?' He ignored my questions and asked one of his own. As it happened, I hadn't heard of any such thing, but I'd once read a book called *The Third Eye*. As far as I can remember, the writer claimed to be the reincarnation of a Tibetan sage, and after returning to the land of his fathers, he had a tiny hole drilled in his forehead: an aperture through which he could see manifestations of eternal wisdom. Poppycock, but entertaining reading and the book sold a hell of a lot of copies.

It sold a lot more when the author was accused of being an impostor who'd never been anywhere near Tibet.

'We are dealing with a similar illusion, Bill.' Brown had resumed familiar terms and he looked at the loungers on the forward deck again. 'My guests are quiet and tractable at the moment because they believe they have been given the power of the Third Ear. A spiritual receiver picking up orders and making promises for good behaviour. I suspect that what they hear is self-induced and, during their confinement in the camp, they developed some kind of group telepathy. It is also likely that the drugs I administered to keep them quiet may be partly responsible, though I am a physician, not a psychiatrist.' It was interesting to know that there was something Mr Brown wasn't, but I was impatient for him to get to the point, so I said so.

'I am coming to it, Bill.' He was still watching Sir Jonathan and Miss Cato and the Mackays. 'These people are harmlessly insane at present, and we must foster their insanity. That is why I persuaded them to keep their heads shaven and issued them with outlandish clothes. Why I promised them that they are on their way to a religious settlement where they can spend their days in repentance and meditation. As long as their delusions continue and they are not provoked, we have nothing to fear from them, but what do you think would happen if those imaginary voices ceased for good? What would become of us if their original personalities returned and they guessed what we had in store for them?'

I didn't need a computer to answer that. It would be our turn to suffer a spot of torment and learn obedience. A really savage beating to ensure that we didn't step out of line and the yacht would head for the nearest country that welcomed fugitives from justice. When that country was reached and we were no longer of value, the next beating would be lethal and beddie-byes for the three of us.

'Quite so.' I had said my piece and was rewarded with a flash of Brown's dentures. 'However, that prospect is not as grim as you suppose. Though we are outnumbered three to one, I have an automatic pistol, as you know.' Naturally I knew. He'd been pointing it at me not so long ago.

'No, Bill, a gradual return to normality is the least of my worries. With only a couple of men we can run the yacht efficiently enough and our assistants would work at gunpoint or with a knife at their backs, while the others are battened down in the hold.' He turned from the window and smiled at Peggy. 'I'm sure that you would prove a tower of strength if the need arose, my dear.'

'There's nothing wrong with my strength.' She smirked back at him. Peggy is a staunch supporter of Women's Lib and justifiably proud of her physique. Once, when her ex-husband's ship was in port, a crew member came lurching back from some quayside dive and made a pass at her. If he'd been a young and presentable officer, clean, white and twenty-one, she might have responded to his advances, but he wasn't. The sot was a middle-aged Lascar stoker, as black as the ace of spades, as tight as a tick and reeking of stale rum. Peggy has a strong sense of protocol; she believes in keeping inferiors in their proper places and the joker's place was not up on the boat deck, trying to kiss her and calling her his 'shy, white dove'. She grabbed the seat of his pants and tipped him over the side, into the dock. Unfortunately for the stoker, it was a dry dock and the ensuing fall knocked out his front teeth and broke three ribs and a collar-bone. Fortunately for Peg, the scuffle occurred in Sydney and Australians admire athleticism. The jury dismissed the assault charge against her in ten minutes flat and she got complimented by the judge for a plucky defence of her honour. Her would-be ravisher got three years for attempted rape.

'But if they did revert to type ... ?' Peggy had got up to join Brown at the window and the smirk faded. Sozzled stokers were one thing, perverted psychopaths quite another, and she was probably imagining the grip of Jonathan Blake's fingers around her neck. She need not have worried on that score. Sir Jonathan's victims had all been under fourteen and Peg would never see forty again.

'A possibility we must face, Margaret, but there is something much worse.' Brown watched Brian Mackay move lazily across to the rail. 'Bad human beings can be controlled by force and cunning — tortured animals cannot. They must be put down before they savage their masters and the animals in question are too valuable to destroy. We have to deliver them in good shape.

'Physical pain and unendurable mental terror is the problem we must face, Bill.' I had raised my eyebrows and Brown's schoolroom manner returned. 'Psyolibin K, the drug I administered, remains in the system for approximately three weeks and then minor doses must be administered till the subject is gradually weaned of his addiction. Without those doses, the withdrawal symptoms are rather repulsive. The pituitary gland becomes inflamed, the heart and lungs speed up and the patient's anguish is virtually unbearable. He becomes a tortured fiend whose one urge is to revenge his sufferings on others, and the key point is this. After the three weeks I mentioned, there is no warning when the change will appear.'

'But you said that minor doses of the drug will prevent that change.' What Brown had divulged was unpleasant, to put it mildly, and a number of images crossed my mind. I saw myself at the wheel with Bruno Kremer; I saw Bruno's expression start to alter, but I didn't see it quickly enough, and before I could jump aside, his flailing hand would have broken my neck. I thought of being down in the engine-room and watching the Mackays rush me. I imagined a lot of things, but I wasn't unduly worried about sudden outbursts of mania. It was still a return to normality that scared me.

'You're a doctor of medicine, Brown,' I said. 'You administered the drug knowing what the withdrawal symptoms are like, and you must have brought supplies of the stuff along to prevent those symptoms recurring.'

'Naturally, and I was prepared for everything except Jones's death and the collision with your launch.' He opened another cupboard and I saw that the cover of a deckhead lamp was broken and its heavy glass lens had fallen on to a rack of bottles and phials. 'My store of Psysolibin K, or what remains of it.' He held up a shattered container to show a single drop of liquid left in its base. 'This might ... just might, be enough to put a small baby to sleep.'

' "The best-laid schemes o' mice and men gang aft a-gley".' His Teutonic attempt to reproduce a lowland Scots dialect was ludicrous, but I was not amused. The prospect ahead was too grim for humour. In a few days time, nine men and women might suddenly go berserk and turn on us. There would be no warning, and locking them up in the hold would defeat our purpose, as Brown was to explain.

'Without strait-jackets to restrain them, they'd either tear each other to pieces or brain themselves against the bulkheads and the *Pandora* contains no restraining devices. Nor have we any tranquillizers now, thanks to you.' He looked sadly at the broken glass and closed the cupboard door. 'Nobody will pay rewards for corpses, I'm afraid, and our only hope is to get to England on schedule, before the withdrawal symptoms start.'

He was wrong. It wasn't our only hope and I told him so loudly and clearly and with feeling. Leonia was a damn sight nearer than England and the obvious bet was to get there and throw ourselves on the mercies of Hurst-Hutchins.

'That is out, Bill. Definitely and utterly and completely out, because President Hurst-Hutchins would merely claim the rewards himself and send us packing.' He nodded at his right arm and I saw that the pistol was still lodged in the sling. 'I am in command of this vessel and it is my firm intention to deliver my passengers back where they belong and in ample time. You have both agreed to my terms and I would strongly advise you to stick to our bargain.'

Little Mr Brown fancied he'd got the whip-hand and it appeared that his fancy was justified. His plan, and the way he'd seen through mine, proved that he was a clever person. His determination to press on after losing his mate and with only a crew of deranged amateurs to sail the ship showed that he was a damn fine seaman and abnormally courageous. I looked at a calendar on his desk, I looked at a barometer with its needle steady at 'set fair', I listened to the healthy beat of the engines and I decided to play ball.

For a time that was; £25,000 is a handy sum, but

it's only a tenth of a quarter million and that was what I wanted. Nor did I trust Mr Brown. Once we sighted Dear Old Blighty and our usefulness ended, Peggy and I might follow Jones's example and take a header into one of the props. Before we neared the English Channel, I'd make another radio call and the message would be addressed to Benjamin Easter, Esq. at the Public Prosecutor's Office. Brother Ben was a staunch supporter of law and order and the Royal Navy or the coastguards would be ready and waiting to welcome the *Pandora* home. Mr Brown and his mate with the secluded Sussex mansion weren't going to collar the rewards. Mr William Easter and Mrs Margaret Tey were.

An excellent arrangement and I could only see one snag. Would we get back to Dear Old Blighty in one piece?

10

The long voyage home proceeded and I've never known time pass more slowly than it did in those first few days, though I had plenty to do. Mr Brown's concussion had affected his sense of balance slightly and the yacht was not fitted with stabilizers. As we forged north and the weather started to freshen, the *Pandora* rolled like a hog in a mud bath and he found ladders difficult to negotiate. Peg and I were kept hard at it, checking the course and the log and tending the engines.

Fortunately, Brown's faith in those engines was justified. Twin diesels constructed by Messrs Samuel Haddock & Son of Walker-upon-Tyne, which kept pounding happily away at just under their maximum revs. There were no knocks, no overheating, no misbehaviour at all and I often raised a convivial mug of tea to toast the founder of the firm that built 'em. Old Sam Haddock had probably been a typical Bible-thumping Victorian slave-driver, but he had set a tradition of quality and craftsmanship and his successors had carried it on.

But, though the yacht and her machinery gave no trouble, every minute seemed like an hour and every hour a day. Our companions were always in our thoughts and Peggy and I watched them like hawks while we worked, and listened to them whenever we were idle. During joint off-duty periods, we kept a wedge hammered under the cabin door, and though Peg claimed to sleep soundly, I could only doze in short snatches. Mr Brown had assured us that the withdrawal symptoms would not start before the 21st of the month, but every footstep in the alleyway, every unusual creak of timbers woke me up and I reached for a fire-axe I'd positioned below my bunk. I'd also obtained a useful sheath knife from the carpenter's stores and it never left my side.

Nor did fear lessen when I was on watch, and the nights were the worst to bear. Clear nights in particular when there wasn't a cloud in sight and the moon was up. I don't know if there really is a link between the moon and lunacy, but I did know that we were surrounded by dangerous lunatics who might go off the handle without warning. The moonbeams sparkling on the water might have appeared romantic to less anxious eyes, but they gave me the horrors. I counted the hours like a prisoner awaiting reprieve or execution, I looked longingly at any passing vessels that appeared on the horizon, I crossed my fingers in the hope that those valiant old engines would get me to safety in time. I thought of the fun-loving mate's plunge into the screw and kept a civil tongue in my head.

Not that our crew-cum-passengers' manner had altered. They remained meek and biddable and withdrawn and shaved their heads daily with an electric razor Mr Brown had thoughtfully provided; I used it myself from time to time. They performed their duties as well as could be expected and before the crunch came they only worried me on two occasions.

The first incident took place during a four-to-eight morning watch. Brown was in his quarters, Peggy had command of the ship and I was trying to take an uneasy nap when she came hurrying down to our cabin and gave the *rat-ter-tat* recognition signal we always used.

She didn't look anxious when I opened the door; more puzzled and annoyed, and I soon discovered why. On reaching the deck, I saw that the spectacle we had witnessed after our arrival was on display again. Our helpers had deserted their posts and their bunks and were on their knees again, either engaged in group prayer or listening to their mysterious voices. Voices which appeared to have a practical as well as a spiritual intelligence behind them. Before joining the meeting, Brian Mackay had slowed the engines to a safe cruising speed and Ted Langdon had lashed the wheel to keep the *Pandora* roughly on course. The session was only a short one. After a few minutes, normality returned and the next cause for alarm did not take place till the ship was approaching the Bay of Biscay.

The fuel tanks were getting low and, as the sea was calm, Brown and I decided to broach half the reserve drums. A hose was connected to a pump and led to the hold; the pump was primed and Bruno Kremer and I opened the drums. The operation commenced smoothly.

The drums each held twenty gallons of diesel oil, but one could not drain them completely, and the dregs had to be collected later. If air was sucked into the hose, the pump would lose its suction effect and more priming would be needed. I explained that carefully to Bruno Kremer and told him to be sure to close the hosecock as soon as one drum was almost empty and then transfer the nozzle to the next. He said he understood; three containers were successfully dealt with and I was idly looking around the hold and wondering who the benches against the bulkheads were intended for, when I heard noises. First a rumble, then a sort of sighing belch, finally a light sucking, gurgling sound. Air was being drawn into the pipeline, the pump priming would soon be lost and I bellowed at Bruno to close the tap and be quick about it.

My words went unheeded. Bruno was crouched over the drum with a dazed look in his eyes, so I yelled at him again and then shoved him aside, pulled the hose out of his hands and turned off the tap.

'You ... Bill ... You pushed me.' The dazed expression had vanished and his eyes were furious. 'You dared to jostle and shout at me, you insubordinate bastard, and I don't like being pushed around by employees.' His fists were clenched and I reached for my sheath knife, suspecting the worst. Piety had gone to the winds, reason had returned and Bruno was his old, obnoxious self. The knife was out of its scabbard and he was squaring up at me when another character change occurred.

'Yes — yes — I hear you.' He screamed as though electric shocks were wracking him. 'I hear you clearly, so please — please don't hurt me again.' I hadn't touched a bristle of his shaven scalp, but the knife blade might have been digging into his ribs already and he drew back gasping. 'Please don't be angry, Bill. Please forgive me.' His body seemed to shrink inside the robe and his fists unclenched.

'It's hot in the hold, Bill; hot and airless and I didn't know what I was doing or realize who you were.' His tone was abject, but the lies were barefaced, because he'd spoken my name and remembered that I'd once worked for him. I felt like killing him then and there and not only for the sake of 'Auld Lang Syne'. Bruno Kremer had regained his sanity for a brief period and the next return might last a deal longer. He was a public danger and his death would not beggar anybody. The £10,000 on his head was chicken-feed compared to Sir

Jonathan Blake's and Sally Lambert's price tags.

'I'm sorry, Bill, so very sorry.' His hands hung limply at his side, he was a sitting duck and I decided to let him have it through the heart. 'For God's sake accept my apologies and don't hurt me, Bill.'

'Mr Easter *does* accept them, Kremer.' Bruno was almost grovelling at my feet, but it was a brisk, commanding voice from above which made me lower the knife.

'Now, both of you had better come to your senses and get back to work.' Mr Brown had witnessed the altercation and he was leaning over the hatch with his hearing-aid in position. He appeared to have realized my intentions and he was a miserly man who valued all his merchandise. It also appeared that he had recovered the use of his injured arm. The sling was missing, the automatic was firmly clenched in his right hand and the muzzle was pointing at me.

Two events; one trivial and one unnerving, but they were both preludes to the main act which was far more serious. It was bloody terrifying, bloody painful and it bloody near cost me my life. As one might expect, Peggy's bloody-mindedness set the ball rolling.

The days passed, the ship sailed on and the weather kept changing. We had choppy seas off the Canaries, where the last of the flying fish disappeared and other creatures took their place. Then Madeira screened in mist off the starboard beam and finally blue skies again. The water as smooth as glass and our new companions plunging along beside us. Beak-nosed dolphins, the sailors' friends, leaping and diving and dancing and urging us home.

Europe was abreast at last and my fears had started to diminish. Our schedule was being maintained, there had been no more untoward happenings since the business in the hold, and everyone was civil as pie. Mutual trust was the order of the day and I waited for an opportunity to radio Brother Ben and get him to alert the authorities of our approach.

'I give you my word that I would merely have fired a warning shot, Bill.' Mr Brown had assured me of that, with his lips grinning and eyes as dead as marbles, and I accepted his word up to a point — a narrow point. Peggy and I were still of use to him, but our usefulness was lessening because his protégés were starting to learn their new trade. At a pinch, he could probably manage without us and we had to mind our Ps and Qs till my radio-message started the wheels turning and the navy hove into sight. A noble sight it should be — 'Ready, aye ready ... Steady, boys, steady'. Grim, grey warships with guns loaded and boarding parties lined-up.

After that meeting, I'd tell Mr Brown exactly what I thought of him, but, for the moment, a spot of forelock-pulling was necessary. I apologized for brandishing the knife and I grinned as I shook his hand and said that there were no hard feelings and I rather enjoyed having pistols pointed at me. Mr Brown did not grin back. He was the kind of man who only appreciates his own jokes, but he'd have one to put him in stitches soon, and put him behind bars too. Peg and I would have the last laugh and we'd split our sides while we counted the reward money.

I was considering that cheerful moment when the third incident started. Brown and Peggy were on duty; she in the engine-room, he on the bridge, and I'd rigged a hammock by the stern and was taking my ease.

Nobody was in sight, I was quite alone and for the first time since we'd joined the *Pandora*, I felt completely relaxed. I switched on a little transistor radio I'd found in the saloon and listened to the news from England. There'd been an air disaster in Japan, a block of flats had collapsed in Dublin, a Royal Duke had bust his thigh playing polo; all the usual tales of woe.

An M.C.C. touring side had been whipped by the West Indies, a cabinet minister had been whipped by a call-girl, delegates for that damn silly ecumenical conference had started to arrive in London. Nothing of any interest, so I tuned in to a concert and closed my eyes. When I opened them, the music had stopped and I had a companion.

'I've brought you a few presents, Bill.' Sally Lambert had switched off the radio and she was smiling down at me. Her eyes were almost the exact opposites of Mr Brown's — huge and lustrous, and they seemed to glow with warmth and affection.

'These are not what you're used to I'm afraid, but I do hope you'll enjoy them.' She held out a cardboard box, but I didn't take it from her and those come-hither eyes did not fool me. They had once persuaded an old man to produce his bearer bonds and eat a tasty dish of powdered glass. *La Belle Lambert* had been a fun-loving girl before Asmonda's merry men went to work on her and like Bruno Kremer she might also be about to revert to type. For all I knew, the box could house a plague-carrying rat or a Black Widow spider which she encouraged to bite people. At the same time, she really was *belle* in spite of her shaven scalp and dreary habit and I felt lust starting to rear its ugly head.

'There's no need to be frightened, Bill.' Though their

eyes differed, she appeared to share Mr Brown's mind-reading abilities. 'I rolled them myself with tissue-paper and flour-paste and they can't possibly harm you. Please try one ... Pretty please.' She opened the box and I sat up with a jerk. No rat, no spider — but cigarettes. About a hundred cigarettes; hand-rolled as she had said, but rolled by an expert. They looked as firm as factory products and ten times more tempting because I was craving for a smoke.

'Thank you ... thank you very much.' The box also contained matches and I lit one of her gaspers and inhaled deeply.

Gasper was correct and I gasped. I coughed and heaved and damn near brought up my last meal; vegetable soup and fat-free dumplings. The cigarette tasted like old rope, which was not surprising. The main ingredient was old rope, though various herbs had been added to give a suggestion of nicotine. A disgusting blend, but I was so smoke-starved that I risked another drag.

'Not bad — quite palatable, in fact.' My lungs were getting accustomed to the stuff and I beamed at the donor. 'You're an extremely kind and clever woman, Miss Lambert.'

'Also extremely lonely, Bill.' Though it's difficult for someone to be alluring when she's hairless and dressed in a sort of sack, my benefactress managed it. 'But do call me Sally, Bill ... much more friendly.'

'Why not, Sally.' I nodded and she squatted down on a folded tarpaulin, smiling like a slave girl whose sole ambition is to please Massa. By some female guile, she had hitched her robe up to reveal an expanse of thigh and my Caliban lust rose accordingly. She had nice legs — long and slim and white and I was sure that the rest of her body would match them. A welcome change from Peg's bloated, sunburnt charms.

I fought lust. Sally Lambert was giving me a clear welcome-home look, but she was tainted and bent as they come. She was dynamite and not for me, however much I fancied her, and I pulled at the cigarette and considered what had happened to some Biblical chaps who yielded to temptation. Adam being booted out of Eden, Samson losing his strength on account of Delilah, Joseph...

No, not Joseph. He was the stubborn one, the virtuous one, who kept his head and his self-control. Joseph told Potiphar's wife exactly where she got off and ended up top man in the Land of Egypt.

'Come down here beside me, Bill.' She crooked a finger and leaned back on the canvas. The movement pulled her outlandish garment still higher and I was sure she was bollock-naked beneath it. 'A hammock's very nice for one person, but a bit cramped for two. I know — I've tried it.'

I bet she had. Little Miss Lambert must have tried everything; she'd be an excellent playmate, but she wasn't having it off with me, thank you very much. I wasn't bedding down with a nut who might scratch my eyes out while I laid her and I kept my mind fixed on Joseph. Clean-living, virtuous Joseph, whose celibacy earned him the patronage of Jehovah and the Pharaoh.

'Please Bill ... pretty please.' She repeated the invitation and I glanced around the deck. The coast was clear, Mr Brown was still upon the bridge, Peggy in the engine-room, and the quotation 'Hell has no fury like a woman scorned' occurred to me. Sally Lambert was crazy about me and she and Mavis Cato were in charge of the cooking. She might scratch my face if I gave in to temptation, but she could do something a damn sight worse if I rejected her advances, and a dose of splintered bamboo would not offend her vegetarian principles. I shrugged Joseph aside, flicked the cigarette over the rail and joined her on the canvas. The fun was at its height when all hell broke loose.

I believe Roman Catholic priests still advocate *coitus interruptus* as a method of birth control and more fool they. It's a harmful practice which can injure the nervous system and I learned that to my cost. My nerves were in a shocking state already and our *coitus* was interrupted suddenly, violently and brutally. I was knocked cold.

At first, I imagined that the ship's siren was blaring out a warning. Secondly, that the *Pandora* had struck another vessel and the impact had thrown me away from Sally Lambert and slammed my head against the deck. Finally that we'd been swamped by a hurricane.

All wrong. When I opened my eyes, I realized that the siren sound was a bellow of enraged humanity and human hands had torn me from my loved one. Peg had emerged from the engine-room for a breath of fresh air, spotted our frolic and gone on the rampage. She'd propped Sally up against the rail and was beating the daylights out of her.

'Bitch — bitch — lecherous bitch.' Peggy's fists were slamming away as though she was having a workout with a punching bag. 'I'll teach you not to pester my Bill, you foul-minded, lustful, little bitch.'

'Stop it, Peg.' The descriptions of Miss Lambert were apt enough, but there was no need to kill the woman and I staggered to my feet to prevent murder or mayhem. 'Stop it, I say.'

'Leave her alone, damn you.' I grabbed Peggy's arm,

but the intervention came too late and behind my back the *schlop — schlop — schlop* of the propellers reminded me how the mate, David Jones, had paid for his misplaced sense of humour. Mr Brown had suggested that group telepathy was partly responsible for our passengers' behaviour and, though Sally did not cry out, her discomfort had raised the alarm. She had other rescuers; eight of them and they were belting towards us like hounds after a scent. It was Peg's turn to receive a drubbing, or rather be torn to pieces, because they were all armed. Bruno Kremer had an axe, Jonathan Blake a boat-hook, Tim Mackay a bottle which he smashed against a stanchion without slackening his pace. The rest were provided with marlin spikes and belaying-pins and knives, and I realized that Peggy was not their only quarry. They imagined I'd also been maltreating their little buddy and were coming at me as well as her.

My own knife was in my overall pocket and I had discarded the overalls. There was no time to reach them because the assault had begun. Peggy squealed as Sir Jonathan stabbed her arse with the boat-hook and Bruno's axe was flailing out at my head. I ducked under the blade, pulled Bruno towards me and planted a knee in his groin. A hard knee which made him drop the axe and go spinning sideways into Blake. They both collapsed in a heap, but the odds against us were too great. Peg was on the deck with Cornford, the kidnapper, crouched over her with a knife in his hand. Fingers were clutching my neck from behind. Tommy Powell had slammed at me with a belaying-pin and missed, Mavis Cato was also provided with a broken bottle. Just before Powell lunged out again and found his target, I saw the jagged glass glint in the sunlight. I saw Mavis Cato's face.

A blackmailer's face and an attractive one. Firm, even features implying honesty. Full lips suggesting a warm, kindly nature. Calm, grey eyes to inspire trust. Miss Cato's face had charmed the daylights out of her victims, but it did not charm me. It frightened me more than the thing she was about to slash into my own face, because it was completely and utterly empty.

I could have accepted anger. I'd have understood sadism, lust, revenge or the urge to protect a friend. I'd have condoned the smug look with which one swats a fly, even though I was the fly in question. But I could not accept negation and that was what I saw.

Mavis Cato's face was as expressionless as a death mask — as blank as a wax image. All their faces were, and in one split second I knew why. Mr Brown was right about the group telepathy. That had summoned them to Sally Lambert's rescue, but he was wrong in saying that Asmonda's brainwashing had been incomplete. The course had been completed all right and proved 100 per cent effective. Mavis Cato's arm was flexed, Cornford's knife was poised over Peggy's heart, Powell's belaying-pin was swinging towards my head. Peg and I were going to die, but men and women would not kill us. Our murderers were machines and some third force controlled them.

11

'He's a good fellow and 'twill all be well.' I've always been a fan of Omar Khayyám and that promise was the first thing to re-enter my thoughts. My god really was a good fellow, he'd turned up trumps as usual and carried me off to paradise. I was being rocked on a soft, comfortable couch, the sky around me had a rosy, twilight hue and a shadowy female figure, probably an angel, was caressing my forehead with soothing fingers. 'The strife was o'er, the battle done' for Mr Easter and I felt at peace with the universe.

'Open your eyes, Bill. I saw them flicker just now, so open them properly and look at me. Open them, I say.' The spell in paradise was short-lived, the caresses stopped and I received a stinging slap across the cheek. When I did open my eyes, I saw their lids had produced the twilight effect. A glaring deckhead lamp was blazing over me, the couch was my hard, uncomfortable bunk and the sea was responsible for the rocking motion. Nor had I any angel in attendance. Peggy was at my side and it was she who had delivered the slap.

'Of course we're not dead, you bloody fool — at least not yet.' I was still only half-conscious and she frowned at the question and dragged me up into a sitting position. 'For Christ's sake come to your senses, Bill. Can't you remember what happened?'

I remembered. The image of that broken bottle returned with a rush and sent me staggering from the bunk to the wash-basin mirror. My sight had not been affected, but I take pride in my appearance and I dreaded what the mirror might reveal, though there was no need for anxiety. Mavis Cato had either missed or stayed her hand and, apart from a bruise on the forehead and a thick growth of stubble, I looked in fair working order. I turned on a tap, sluiced my face with water and questioned Peggy again.

'They were going to kill us, darling, and God knows what stopped them.' Peggy is a great one for taking the Lord's name in vain. 'Powell belted you with a belaying-pin and that fellow Cornford had a knife over me. I was so scared that I couldn't move a muscle. I just lay waiting to die and then something stopped him stabbing me. The knife dropped out of his hand and he smiled.'

'Cornford smiled?' That hardly seemed likely and I recalled those set, inhuman expressions while I dried my face.

'A sort of smile, but I only just came round myself a few minutes ago and everything's a bit vague.' Peggy lowered herself on to the bunk, planting her weight on her left buttock because Blake's jab with the boathook must have made the right one a bit painful. 'A sad, pleading sort of smile it was, like a kid trying to get round you for a favour. And his voice was sad too. "Sorry, my dear," he said, speaking ever so gently. "Don't want to hurt you but I must ... must obey her ... her orders." He broke off in a stammer and then clenched his fist and hit me under the chin. That's all I know, Bill. I was knocked out cold and when I came to, I was lying here in the dark. I thought I was alone till I heard you snoring away beside me, and switched on the light.'

Peggy was obviously as confused as myself because

I don't snore. What she had heard were the groans of the yacht which was pitching and tossing like an unbroken horse trying to escape from its bridle. All the same, her news was encouraging, because it suggested that the withdrawal symptoms from Mr Brown's drug had not provoked our attackers. Concern for Sally Lambert had triggered them off and once they saw — realized — understood ... How does one describe the perception of telepathic maniacs? Once they were sure Sally was safe, benevolence returned. Cornford had apologized before putting Peggy to sleep, Mavis Cato had not used the bottle and Tommy Powell had gone fairly easy with his belaying-pin. I looked at myself in the mirror again and saw that the skin was unbroken and the bruise had already started to fade.

'Where are they, Peg?' I listened to the familiar shipboard noises and realized that two were missing. The engines had stopped and there was no sound of human activity. Though I felt dazed and exhausted and longed to return to my bunk, I forced myself to stagger to the door and pull it open.

Night — a thick, drizzly night with quite a heavy sea running, and apart from our cabin, the *Pandora* was in darkness. Even the navigation lights were out and at first I could hardly see anything. Then a pale, watery moon slid out from a belt of cloud and I saw that there was no one on the bridge and the yacht was at anchor. Also, that the big motor lifeboat was missing and its lowering tackle still dangling from the davits. Mr Brown and his rats appeared to have deserted their floating home and I couldn't imagine why. The *Pandora* was perfectly seaworthy and Brown's destination was England — his pal's secluded haven on the Sussex coast. Unless Peggy and I had been unconscious for several days, which seemed unlikely, they were still a long way from journey's end.

But everything made sense if Bruno and the others had regained their own senses and rumbled Brown. If they'd realized he was no pious benefactor, but a hard-headed businessman out for the reward monies, John Brown's body would be drifting on ocean's bosom and his charges heading for Spain or Portugal in the lifeboat.

A possible solution, but there was no time for guesswork. Lights — the lights of a big ship were approaching on the starboard beam and a second vessel was coming up astern of us. I could also see a beacon flashing away on the horizon and read its call sign. One long red flash — two short yellows — a longish white. The *Pandora* had been anchored in a busy shipping lane and a collision was imminent unless we revealed our presence and quick about it. I yelled at Peggy to follow me and ran for the upper deck like a mountain hare on scree.

I only just got there in time. Another cloud had obscured the moon and, after switching on the bridge and navigation lights, the first thing I saw was the cliff-like bow of an unladen oil-tanker towering over us. She sheered off in the nick of time with an agonized whistle-hoot, and the hoot was followed by storms of Scandinavian abuse from a loud hailer. I think the language was Norwegian, though I only know a few words of the lingo. But the tone of the officer on watch made his meaning clear enough, so I shouted back and asked him what was wrong with his bloody radar. I shouldn't think he heard the inquiry and I didn't really care. Sticks and stones may break my bones, but names can never hurt me.

'I found this, Bill.' Peggy had come puffing up the

companionway. 'It was pinned to a bulwark in the cabin.' She held out an envelope, but I ignored her and stared at the beacon. I felt I should recognize its signal, but imagined my eyes or my brain were deceiving me, because lighthouses are stationary, soundly constructed buildings and they don't wander around the world at will. I timed the flashes and then took a pilot guide from the chart-room locker. As I flicked through the book, I thought of my unshaven chin and when I found the correct page, my left arm started to throb. After checking the reference, I knew the cause of that throbbing. I knew damn-near everything and my flesh crawled.

One red impulse of four seconds' duration — two yellow, one-second impulses — one white, three-second impulse. I was correct in thinking that lighthouses do not move from place to place. But ships move and the *Pandora* had sailed a long way since Powell clouted me with the belaying-pin. I closed the guide and studied the line of punctures on my arm. The marks of a hypodermic needle that had kept me asleep for over three days. The beacon swirling away through the scud was Havelock Head and Havelock Head was in dear old, sunny Sussex-by-the-Sea.

'Mr Easter and Mrs Tey.' I had opened the envelope Peg found in the cabin and saw that Mr Brown had once more reverted to a formal address.

'I regret that we have to part company without verbal farewells and do apologize for putting you under sedation.' I had had goose pimples before I started to read the letter and the last two words of the sentence made me squirm. I thought of the drug Brown had given to his prodigals and the withdrawal symptoms that followed it, and only one factor gave me a glimmer of hope. Psysolibin K made its subjects obedient and tractable and I didn't feel either of these qualities. I felt like rooting Mr Brown up the arse with a steel boot.

'However, let me assure you that your coma was produced by a mild morphine derivative and you will suffer no ill-effects.' The assurance did not lessen my anxiety, because Mr Brown had told us he was out of sedatives. He was a liar with a keen sense of humour and completely untrustworthy.

'The injections you received were given in your own interests, as I am sure you will agree when you consider the situation calmly.

'My protégés are an unstable lot, as you have already learned. Though they spared you on that last occasion, I feared that you might offend them again and be less fortunate, and thought it best that you should be confined to your quarters for your own safety.'

Like hell he did. Mr Brown's own safety was his worry and he considered Peggy and I were trouble-makers. He also considered, and quite rightly, that he no longer needed us. His crew were partially trained and he'd gambled on completing the voyage without our help. If the engines played up, or the weather got really bad, we'd probably have been given some stimulant to spur us into action again. The little swine had had the best of both worlds and there was only one question to be asked. Why hadn't he killed us before making off in the boat?

'Now, as to the future.' The notepaper was small; Brown had a large, flamboyant hand and I turned to the second page. 'The arrangement was that you should be paid a share of our friends' reward money in return for your assistance. Your foolishness has made that assistance unacceptable to me and I am afraid our agreement is no longer in force.

'But I am a fair-minded man and do not wish you to go empty-handed.' Fair-minded, my foot! He knew that if we did go empty-handed, I'd follow him to the ends of the earth and he had to give us some sort of cut.

'Your original intention was to take the *Pandora* to Leonia and sell her, and this is what I now suggest.' He appeared to have changed his mind about scuttling the yacht and I raised my eyebrows at the next passage.

'Though Constitution is no longer a feasible port of call, unless you can obtain more fuel and engage a crew, there should be plenty of European buyers on the market. You will require deeds of ownership, naturally, but that should be a small problem to people with your considerable talents.' A true statement, though unhelpful. We had plenty of talents, but forgery was not one of them.

'When you both visited my quarters the other day, Mr Easter suspected that some person was stationed in the alleyway or the night-cabin, and he was quite correct.'

'That person is to be found in the cabin and she is the legal owner of this vessel. She is also completely in your power, so try to persuade her to sign the yacht's deeds over to you. The task should not be difficult.' That was that, though Mr Brown signed himself, 'Yours sincerely' and added a postscript that he had thought it necessary to render the radio transmitter inoperative.

She is the legal owner ... she is completely in your power. The implications raised a fresh crop of goose pimples.

A woman was locked in that cabin. A helpless woman, bound to the bunk or drugged to the eyeballs, and

Brown's suggestion was that we tortured the poor old cow to gain legal ownership of the *Pandora*. I wasn't going to have any hand in that — not for all the tea in China or the gold in Fort Knox. Judges deal out heavy sentences for torture; the heaviest that the law allows.

But Peggy might yield to temptation — yes, she definitely might. I studied her expression while she read the letter and an attractive possibility occurred to me. Why *poor old cow*? Maybe the prisoner was a young and lithe and adorable millionairess. Sleeping Beauty waiting for Prince Charming's kiss, who would reward her rescuer with more than a battered yacht and filthy lucre.

I was still looking at my portly heart's delight and she was no oil painting. I thought of her selfish greed on the dinghy and the pangs of hunger it had caused me. I remembered that Peg's incompetence had beggared me, and her attack on Sally Lambert had almost cost me my life. I didn't owe Peg one scrap of loyalty and there was a more tempting fish to fry. I walked out of the chart-room to claim my reward.

Brown's injections and the effort of running up to the bridge had left me incapable of clear thought and I felt the same rosy haze I'd experienced in the cabin. To my stupid, numbed mind, the future seemed assured and equally rosy. The sleeping princess would awaken with my kiss.

12

Primitive man possessed inborn warning devices which most present-day human beings have lost. But a few fortunate individuals still have them and I'm one of those fortunates. I knew we were in danger before my physical senses registered a thing.

I had just opened the door of Mr Brown's quarters when the warning came and it was as clear as a flashing lamp, as loud as an alarm bell. I had no idea what the threat was, but it made me stop dead in my tracks, holding the door ajar and craning into the state-room. Mr Brown was not only a liar and a crook; like his defunct mate he had a perverse sense of humour and I could see his lips smiling, I could hear his laughter, I could smell...

The odour which usually pervaded the *Pandora* was composed of brine and bilge water, mildew and diesel oil and boiled vegetables. An objectionable pong, though not a disturbing one, but two elements were being added; smoke and hot fumes. The yacht was on fire and the cause of the fire was apparent. A switch had been screwed to the door frame and there was a wire leading away from the switch. When I'd opened the door an electric spark must have ignited a cache of inflammable material; cellulose or petrol-soaked rags and the blaze had begun.

A considerable blaze already, and spreading fast.

Smoke was visible now and the sound of the flames was increasing at every second. The ship's inner timbers were old and dry and they were starting to burn like matchwood.

'Not yet, Peg.' She was tugging at my arm and screaming out the call for retreat, but I ignored her, though I could feel the deck growing warm beneath my feet. Mr Brown had planned to kill us, but he could have spoken the truth on one point. There might be a woman in the night-cabin and my dazed Sir Galahad mood was still in the ascendancy. By hook or by crook, I was determined to save her.

'What are you waiting for, Bill?' I was trying to pull away from Peggy, but she has the grip of a gorilla and held on to me. 'Come to your senses, because we've got to get out of here and launch the rubber dinghy.'

'Not yet, Peggy.' A dull detonation shook the yacht as one of the fuel drums exploded and I saw that the state-room door was not only closed by a spring, it was self-locking and the lock had been reversed. A key would be needed to open it from inside and, if Peg and I had gone through that doorway, we wouldn't have had a chance in hell. For some reason, Mr Brown wanted to burn us alive and he had planned for everything except my intuition.

'Let go of me, Peggy, or I'll knock you cold and you'll have to wait for the fire to warm you.' I clenched a fist, the threat worked and she released her grasp. 'Now, just stay where you are and keep this door open till I come back.' She nodded and I started off, but time was running out. There was a second muffled explosion in the hold, the roar of blazing timbers grew louder and louder and smoke and tongues of flame were licking up between the deck planking. The atmosphere was so thick that I had to grope my way blindly towards the night-cabin.

I had expected the cabin to be locked and I was right, but Mr Brown had thoughtfully left the key in position. I turned it with my lungs gasping for lack of air and the rubber soles of my boots starting to melt and stick to the deck. I slammed the door open and saw my Sleeping Beauty.

There was far less smoke in the cabin than the stateroom. I could see her clearly, and it was just like the fairy story. She lay on a bed and she was small and slim and very, very lovely. She wore a white tunic, her hair was long and golden, and some kind of silver orb lay between the long, slim hands spread out before her. A princess perhaps, but not the owner of the yacht. She was a girl in her early teens and too young to be the legal owner of anything valuable.

So young, so lovely and so light. Though I was faint with the heat and almost suffocating, I hardly noticed the weight of her body as I picked it up and staggered back through the state-room. So soft too, and so calm and brave. Her skin was as smooth as oiled silk and, though she appeared to be conscious and tears were trickling from her open eyes, her expression showed no fear. None whatever, and, after stumbling past Peg, I knew that smoke was not entirely responsible for my own tears. I've done a lot of bad things in my life, but at last I'd proved myself a self-sacrificing hero. I felt exactly as Galahad would have done if he'd managed to collar the Holy Grail.

Light — soft — calm — brave — smooth. Five pleasant adjectives, but once I'd reached the open deck and the atmosphere cleared, they changed to a single word. My princess was too light, her flesh was too soft and smooth and her expression was too damn calm and brave. Nor was her face tear-stained, and how the hell could it have been? Have you ever seen a glass eye weep? The lady was melting, the only word to describe her was *phoney* and I dropped her metal globe with a curse.

So far, Mr Brown had failed to kill us, but he'd had a bloody good try and his joke would have raised the rafters in a public house frequented by sadists. I'd risked my life to save a sodding wax dummy.

Peggy was wrong about beating a retreat in the dinghy. Its rubber hull had been slashed and the thing was useless to us. Also, the life-jackets along the rail were missing and the second lifeboat had a plank stove in. I had little doubt that the buoyancy tanks would have been removed. Mr Brown was taking no chances. If we escaped the fiery fate he'd planned, he intended us to drown and I made myself a promise. Should we get out of our predicament alive there'd be no running to my brother or the authorities with tales of woe. The reward money could wait till I'd found Brown. And when I found him, by Christ I'd make him scream.

But it seemed that I might have a bit of screaming to do on my own account first. Tall pillars of flame were pouring up through the foreward deck and three more detonations rang out. They were heavier and sharper than the previous ones and fuel oil had not caused them. There were high explosives on board and, as I clutched the rail for support, I realized that our sojourn on Mother Earth might be nearing its end. The water below was not only rough, it had become an inferno. Burning oil had poured out through the *Pandora*'s shattered sides and the sea was covered with fire.

'Over here, Bill.' Peg had made for the stern and I followed her and saw that there was still a narrow, oil-free channel which might take us to safety. Peg had also found a ten-foot length of rope and we lashed the ends around our waists and took a last look at our floating hotel, which would not float much longer. The yacht had become a miniature volcano and we removed our boots, stepped over the rail and took the plunge.

Plunge was not really an accurate way to describe our departure. The hull was so low that we could almost step on to the water. But, unfortunately, we couldn't walk on it and I went in head under and gasped with the sudden cold. My last dip had been in the tropics and I'd forgotten how chilly northern seas can be. It felt as though needles were stabbing at every inch of my body and for a moment, I lost control and floundered helplessly, seeing the flames closing in on three sides. Then the rope around my waist tightened and we were away. Peggy is a much stronger swimmer than I am and doubtless her fat provided insulation against the cold. She struck out with a powerful Australian racing crawl and, though I tried to paddle feebly along behind her, my efforts were negligible. Peggy was the hero of that hour; she kept churning steadily along like a porpoise or the queen of the mermaids — the queen mother. Peg's sterling performance soon put us beyond the ring of fire, but even the strongest swimmer can't compete against a hundred odd tons of metal. There was a sudden deep rumbling noise as though a giant had broken wind, the waves smoothed and the sea started to tilt and run back like a mill race. The weight of the *Pandora*'s machinery had taken her down to *you know who's* locker and suction was dragging us back. When the phenomenon stopped, my toes were within inches of the burning oil and worse trials followed. Missiles broke the surface, shot into the air like arrows and plunged down on us. Loose timbers sent hurtling up from the sea-bed by water pressure and one of them found a target. The rope slackened and I saw that Peggy was floating helplessly beside the plank that had knocked her out.

Before the *Pandora* sank she had been drifting shoreward and the beam on Havelock Head looked fairly close now. Less than a mile away and, though I've never won any cups for swimming, I fancied I could make it on my own. The snag was that I was bound to Peg. Morally, because she had saved me from the fire — physically, because I couldn't untie the rope. I tried to — I tried hard — but my fingers were too numb and I soon gave up. As I'd thought in the dinghy, it seemed to be a question of 'what a beautiful thing it is to lay down one's life for a friend', so I swam over to her and gripped her head in the professional life-saving manner I'd been taught at prep. school.

The trouble was that the instruction had been given in the school swimming pool and my partner was a boy named Philip Bedding who weighed about seven stone. The sea was rough, Peggy could double Bedding's burden and there was no longer a hope of drifting ashore. The tide had turned and we were being carried away from the coast.

My legs kept kicking out as effectively as I could make them, which was not very effectively, because the cold was giving me cramp. After a while, I just accepted defeat and floated. I couldn't drag my load any further, nor could I escape from it. Only death would part me from Peggy and I stared at a beam of yellow moonlight and thought of my lost gold and what a wow of a time I could have had spending the stuff. A happy last thought, which so engrossed me that I never realized the light did not come from the moon and I didn't hear our rescuers till they were almost up to us.

'Steady as she goes, Coxs'n,' said a clipped, Dartmouth College voice. 'Hold her like that and wait for it ... wait I say. Good show. Now, put her to port a trifle. Right, Jenkins, engine astern and smart about it. We don't want to ram the poor devils, do we?'

I should damn well hope they didn't and my heart warmed to the speaker, who had a clear, nautical delivery designed to issue orders in the teeth of a gale. A gentlemanly sailor of the 'England expects' school, rather than the vulgar 'Yo-ho-ho and a bottle of rum' variety.

'The navy's here, old chap, so not to worry, and keep that lass's nose out of the water.' The message was addressed to me and my respect for our saviour increased. 'Before you know it, we'll have you smothered in blankets, soaked in booze and as snug as a bug in a brothel.'

13

I'll say that the navy was there. We'd been picked up by a boat from the minesweeper, H.M.S. *Badger*; Captain W. B. (Whisky Breath) Fenton, and his officers and men were as decent a bunch as one could hope to meet. Peggy was given medical care and, during the short voyage to their base at the Nore, I had a free run of the ship. They accepted that I was too weak and too shocked to answer embarrassing questions, plied me with food and drink and made me feel completely at home.

And not only the fatted calf was laid on. When Fenton noticed that I was about the same size as his first lieutenant, he very kindly told him to lend me a suit of civvy clothes. The garments were handed over with a slightly forced smile and I fancied they were only the lieutenant's second best. But I'm not one to look a gift-horse in the mouth and they fitted me a treat. Peggy was also respectably rigged out when she emerged from the sick-bay. There had been a party during the *Badger*'s last spell in port and, after sampling Whisky Breath's 90° proof export Scotch, a portly W.R.N.S. officer had been carted ashore, wearing nothing but a pair of tights and a bra. Her discarded uniform was still on board and, after the badges of office had been removed, Peggy squeezed into it. She looked like a recruiting poster for Russian prison wardresses.

I have no complaints about the lads on the *Badger*.

They fed us and clothed us and treated us as fellow seafarers who had fallen on evil times. The officers even ordered the lower deck to have a whip-round on our behalf. Though only two pounds and five new pence were contributed, it was a friendly gesture and we expressed suitable gratitude.

No, there's nothing wrong with Her Majesty's Navy, but I'm damned if I can say the same about her civil servants, immigration officials and police who took charge of us after we landed.

'You really expect me to credit this unlikely tale, Easter?' I'd been separated from Peg at the police station and my interrogator was Inspector Dodd; a sunken-cheeked, cadaverous individual who'd been questioning me, on and off, for several hours. 'You still insist that the yacht was called *Pandora*, when no vessel answering the description you have given is listed in any register of shipping?' I'd already said that the name was probably false, but Dodd appeared to lack hearing as well as flesh.

'Now, let us discuss your companions on the vessel again, taking the sinister Mr Brown first.' As I said, I'd decided not to go to the authorities with a tale of woe, and to deal with Brown personally, but the situation had changed. The authorities had tackled me and I'd told Dodd the truth — roughly, of course, and stretching a point here and there.

'Yes, Mr Brown. Or perhaps Mr Black would be a better appellation, Easter. The gentleman appears to be an extremely dark horse.' Dodd grinned, and the two sidekicks assisting him responded appropriately. There was a coarse guffaw from an immigration officer named Manners, though he had none, and a giggle from Miss Violet Wilson, representing the Council for United

Nations' Territorial Security (C.U.N.T.S.). I had no idea why her appropriately named organization was involved, but she was a real busy beaver and had been taking notes throughout the interviews.

'A very dark horse.' Dodd's inventive powers were limited and he repeated himself. 'Brown told you that he was a man of parts; a qualified sea-going engineer, a doctor of medicine and a professional musician. Yet, like his ship, his name is not entered in any of the pertinent lists or reference books. Nor have our inquiries unearthed this elusive hide-out on the Sussex coast, and I would be surprised if they had. Sussex is an overpopulated county these days as I know to my cost. My wife and I have a bungalow in Worthing.' An uninteresting piece of information and I yawned ostentatiously.

'The hide-out appears to be non-existent, so what became of those villains you and Brown intended to deliver to the authorities?' He tapped a pile of photostats on the table. Copies of the faked Leonian death certificates, signed by Colonel M'kimba Wilkins and his venal henchmen. 'I'll tell you what became of them, Easter. They were executed and buried in a common grave several weeks ago and you'll have to spin a better yarn if you don't want to spend the best part of your life in stir.'

'For what crime, Inspector Dog?' Nobody likes a joke about their name and I was pleased to see him wince. 'Mrs Tey and I had the misfortune to be shipwrecked, we were brought ashore without passports, but you can't hold us for that. The records will show that we're British subjects and in any case my brother, Mr Benjamin Easter at the Public Prosecutor's Office, can vouch for me.'

'He already has done, but you are out of date.' Miss Wilson had a prissy, kindergarten-teacher's voice and no best friend to tell her that she suffered from halitosis. '*Sir* Benjamin Easter, K.C.M.G. has been contacted and he made the following statement.' So Brother Ben had got himself on the honours list. All to the good, I thought, though wonders never cease and the award-givers must have scraped the bottom of the barrel.

'This is what Sir Benjamin had to say about you.' The bitch read aloud from her notebook. '"I and the William Easter you describe were born of the same parents and as a Christian I must obey the command to forgive my brother seventy times seven."' Goody, goody, I thought again. We'd never hit it off, but Ben would stand by me and he was an important man. A Knight of the realm, who'd let Dog and Company have it hot and strong.

'"However, 70 multiplied by 7 only totals 490, and, having far exceeded that figure over the years, I no longer consider myself to be my brother's keeper."' The next statement was a body-blow and my faith in Ben crashed.

'"I have not had news of William for a long time and it was my heartfelt hope that he had either died or fled the country on account of some discreditable act which made it unwise for him to return and disgrace his family further. If the man you are holding is indeed my brother, I would suggest that his recent activities be thoroughly investigated and advise you that he is a skilled and cunning liar."'

Judas! Treacherous, hypocritical Judas. No — worse than Judas. Ben had a fat salary and he didn't need any thirty pieces of silver. I don't believe blood's thicker than water — we're lumbered with our families and can choose our friends, but I hadn't suspected that Ben's blood was pure, unadulterated sewage. The grudge-bearing bastard had probably never forgotten a joke I played at his tenth birthday party. A sprinkling of Epsom salts on the Knickerbocker Glories didn't half ruin that festive occasion.

'Fair enough, Miss Wilson,' I said. 'My brother may have disowned me, but the Records Office hasn't and I'm as English as you are. Probably a damn sight more, judging by your complexion.' She had a sallow, yellowish skin which suggested a touch of the tar-brush and the jibe made it even yellower. 'All this cock about a long prison sentence is balderdash and I demand to know why I am being held here and for what reason.'

'Several charges are possible, Easter, and I am quite prepared to outline the situation.' Dodd answered me and he was clearly a man who enjoyed delivering ill-tidings. 'It is my belief that the yacht you refer to as the *Pandora* was in fact the *Helena Trautheim*, and Scotland Yard and the United Nations Organization are rather interested in the *Trautheim*, aren't we, Madam?' He smiled at the Wilson woman and her presence was explained. 'The *Helena Trautheim* is known to have sailed from an East German port some fifteen hours before your ... shall I say *unfortunate shipwreck* and naval units have been looking for her.

'But H.M.S. *Badger* was not one of those units, Easter, and panic is responsible for your predicament. The *Badger* was merely returning from Atlantic exercises, but you considered she might board you and decided to destroy the evidence and sink the yacht with high explosives. *Pandora*, or *Helena* — "what's in a name?"' Dodd fancied himself as a literary cove, but Manners and Mademoiselle Wilson did not respond and I was probably the only one who recognized the quotation.

'I don't know what happened to your associates, Easter. They may have escaped, they may have burned to death, they may have been drowned. But we have you, we know that you are a man of criminal habits and I would like to offer a piece of advice. Stop romancing and tell us where that ship was heading and what her cargo was.' Though I didn't blame him for doubting my story, I yawned a second time. Coppers are like parrots and the only advice they ever give is: Plead guilty and betray your friends.

'The weather is too bad for divers to examine the wreckage at the moment, but it will clear before long — never fear.' Dodd nodded cheerfully at the gusty rain beating against his office windows. 'When that happens, you and Mrs Tey will probably stand trial on some very serious counts, and in the meantime you are to be remanded for the following offences.'

'Being persons suspected of committing a felony on the high seas.' He started to recite the misdeeds with relish. 'Operating a vessel without the proper navigational lights demanded by international law ... wantonly scuttling a vessel to create a hazard to other shipping ... contravening the Immigration Act of 1974 (Section 16C) ...' Our crime sheet appeared to be as long as the accusations Asmonda had made against Bruno Kremer and the social-club members, so I asked if rape, indecent exposure, or buggering a non-consenting male adult were included.

'Not so far, though I wouldn't put anything past you.' Like Brown, the inspector only responded to his own humour and he did not smile. 'Now, let me tell you about the more serious charges which may be preferred after the yacht and her cargo have been examined.'

'Arson ... forgery and falsification of official documents ... murder on the high seas ... plotting to succour the Queen's enemies and overthrow her realm.

'The last is treason, of course.' His skull-like face remained impassive, but the immigration man and C.U.N.T.S. representative nodded approvingly. 'High treason, Easter. One of the three crimes which still carry the death penalty.'

14

Brown ... Brown ... just what had Brown been up to? Pacing one's cell in thought is a cliché, but I paced mine, and I had plenty to think about after Peggy and I were remanded in custody till the police had had time to complete their inquiries. In spite of his grim appearance, Inspector Dodd played the part of a kindly soul during the hearing and he gave me a wink before addressing the magistrates. 'No, your Worships, I have no objection to bail — none at all.' His only stipulation was that, in view of the gravity of the charges, we should each provide a security of £5,000. I could see that the swine wanted to burst out laughing when the request was granted. He knew that we hadn't got a 1,000 pence and no one to cough up for us.

Brown ... Mr John Brown? I was provided with newspapers and allowed to watch television, but no news item helped me. Brown's passengers had not been handed over to the law. They were either dead or hidden away, so why had the man helped them and what was his motive for the rest of the charade? What did the wax dummy signify and why had he tried to burn us alive? If the *Pandora* had been stolen, and that was almost certainly the case, I could see why he wanted to cover his tracks by scuttling her. I could also appreciate that he might have tried to dispose of us if our presence disturbed the penitents' frame of mind and constituted a risk to his own safety.

Fair enough, but why the theatricals? Brown could have disposed of us in a dozen conventional ways and opening the sea-cocks would have sent the yacht quietly down to the bottom. Why the complicated funeral-pyre which gave us a slight chance to escape? Why stage a blazing holocaust that was bound to attract attention and bring other vessels on the scene?

Why — why — why? Sadism — a taste for the dramatic — a malicious sense of humour? From the little I knew of Mr Brown's character, any of those answers might be correct, but I somehow sensed that he had had a more practical reason for our agonized demise and the *Pandora*'s fiery plunge to the deep. But I had no idea what the motivation was and a succession of unwelcome visitors kept interrupting my thoughts.

Inspector Dodd, who'd come into the open and told me what he expected the divers would find when they reached the yacht. The bodies of illegal Pakistani immigrants who'd been battened down in the hold and left to roast or drown when the *Badger* was sighted.

Miss Violet Wilson, who cherished similar suspicions but considered our victims were probably Palestinian Arabs.

The barrister briefed for my defence; a gormless creature, who kept repeating that he could do nothing to help unless I told the truth and collaborated with him.

A Major of the Army Intelligence Corps, who explained Dodd's crack about high treason. In his view the *Pandora* had been chock-a-block with arms and ammunition and we were running them to a most sinister source. An Irish terrorist organization known as the *Clan Eirean na Gael Schintal* which was so ruthless that even the I.R.A. Provisionals shunned its activities.

Four unwelcome visitors who didn't believe a word I said, but the people I wanted to talk to, the gentlemen of the press, were not allowed near me. Dodd was taking no chances that a newspaper would provide bail in return for our story. He had asked the magistrates to conduct the hearing in camera, stating that I and my associates were traffickers in human souls and publicity must be avoided till the case was complete. The sinking of the *Pandora* had been reported, the news of our remand released, but that was all. An unnamed man and woman were assisting the police with their inquiries, the headlines had passed us by. The grapevine had told my fellow prisoners about the treason business, though, and I heard a snatch of disagreeable conversation during an exercise period. 'Who was the last bloke to be 'ung in this country, Syd?' 'Dunno, 'Arry, but I know 'oo the next 'un'll be.'

Brown — Brown — 'You must say Yes to Mr Brown'. The song clicked away in time to my pacing feet. Everyone thought I was mad or a compulsive liar. Nobody believed in Mr Brown's existence. They thought I'd been working for immigrant-smugglers or Irish terrorists, and Brown must have read about that anonymous couple who were helping the police regarding the *Pandora*'s loss. Though he'd failed to kill us, Brown knew we were in trouble and he'd got away scot-free. He was probably laughing his head off at our expense.

But if only I could get out of chokey, he'd stop laughing. Though I had no idea who the man was or how he could be traced, I was quite certain that we'd meet again — that his presence would draw me to him as a magnet tugs at iron.

If I could get out. I stared around the cells. Stone walls do not a prison make, my foot. They certainly help and there'd be no escape for me unless Dodd came to his senses or some well-wisher coughed up the bail money. Though the divers would find no roasted Arabs or Pakistanis in the yacht's remains, the detonations suggested that she had some store of explosives on board and the arms-running charge might stick. Certainly Dodd and his colleagues would try hard to make it stick — bless their kindly little hearts.

CHURCH LEADERS GATHER IN LONDON. I looked away from the gloomy cell walls and picked up a newspaper. The *Daily Globe* was gleeful about the forthcoming ecumenical conference for the simple reason that there was nothing else to be cheerful about. Humanity was at loggerheads as usual, the English cricket team had been soundly thrashed again, and the stock market had fallen. The fact that a flock of cardinals and bishops, Greek Orthodox archimandrites and Free Church moderators were to have a chin-wag was the only cheering news the paper could offer, though it wouldn't cheer any intelligent person. Clerics are as ferocious and self-seeking as the rest of us and that conference would end in an undignified squabble.

Who was it this time? I heard footsteps and a jingle of keys in the corridor and prepared for a visitor. Possibly, the chaplain bringing light literature to while away the idle hours, more probably Dodd or the major to give me another grilling. I turned wearily in preparation for the latter ordeals and then hope sprang eternal to the human breast.

Maybe the Governor with good news. 'Mr Easter, we have done you a grave injustice and must offer our sincere apologies.' The Governor was a courteous, white-haired buffer who might speak like that if the occasion arose.

'The man, Brown, and his associates are under arrest and everything you told the police has been confirmed. The reward monies will naturally be paid to you and

Mrs Tey and you will also receive substantial compensation for wrongful arrest.' I could imagine the old chap clapping me on the shoulder and calling me his *dear boy*. 'That wretched fellow, Dodd, is to be severely reprimanded and reduced to the rank of constable. He'll be pounding a beat soon.'

A pleasant notion, but just as phoney as the sleeping-beauty vision. The door had opened and I saw that my visitor was one of the senior wardens named Robinson.

'Get your coat on please, Mr Easter.' There was no love lost between myself and Robinson, who was a stickler for discipline, and I found the *please* and *mister* disturbing. The date of the trial had been fixed, I was being transferred to a security wing and his politeness was a sort of 'Give the condemned man a hearty breakfast' gesture. I shrugged, put on my jacket and asked him where I was going.

'That is your affair, sir, though you are not to leave the United Kingdom and must report to a police station every forty-eight hours.' He laid some money on my bunk and held out a pen and a clipboard.

'Please sign for your possessions, Mr Easter. Two pounds and five pence which I think you'll find is correct. There was also a sheath knife, but the police are retaining that.'

'You mean that you're releasing me?' I snatched the board from him and scribbled my signature. 'That I'm free?'

'For the time being, sir.' Civility came hard to Robinson, who hated my guts, and his face was as rigid as a graven image. 'You are being allowed out on bail, but it's my belief that you'll soon be back here where you belong.'

'Bail.' It would have been better if the case against

me had been dropped, but I still felt like dancing a jig. Dodd had imagined that nobody would put up the £5,000 and his joke had fallen flat. 'Who handed over the money?'

'It was paid in cash by an agent who is waiting for you with a car, sir.' I could feel Robinson's anger rising like a pressure gauge. 'I do not know the principal's name, Mr Easter, but I can tell you this.' He paused and I waited for the storm to burst.

'The man or woman who has arranged for your release is either a crook or an immoral, irresponsible, do-gooding imbecile.' The thunder roared from his lips and then he remembered I was technically a free man and enforced civility returned. 'Please come this way, Mr Easter. As I said there is a car at the gate for you.'

I couldn't imagine who'd provided the bail, but it was obviously a person of means. The large, impressive Mercedes stationed outside the gate had cost at least three times the sum Dodd had put on me. The uniformed chauffeur who'd presumably delivered the cash was resplendent in gold braid and would have warmed a drill sergeant's heart.

A rather reticent chauffeur though. The glass partition separating us had a speaking grille and when I asked him who his employer was and where we were going, he merely said that the journey would not be long and advised me to press a button on the arm-rest if I required refreshment. The grille clicked shut and that was all I got out of him for a while.

The button operated a panel in the rear of the front seat which slid open to reveal a treasure trove. Bottles and glasses and cups, a cigar case and a flask of coffee.

I ignored the alcoholic beverages, but lit a cigar and poured out some coffee, sampling it with my tongue before drinking. I have a suspicious nature and I'd been doped before. I didn't want that experience repeated and intended to stay on my guard. Somebody had paid £5,000 to bail me out of jail and I didn't know who that somebody was or what his motive could be. He or she might be a rich philanthropist who believed in giving the underdog a square deal, but that seemed improbable. Was Mr Brown or his Sussex friend my benefactor and had I fallen out of the frying-pan and into the fire?

The car itself appeared to confirm that possibility. A nice car — very nice, but the springing felt a trifle heavy for a Merc' and a rap on the window told me why. The glass was a good two inches thick which meant that the body was bulletproof. I tried the door handle and it didn't move a fraction. I'd been abducted by guile and I longed for my cosy prison cell.

'There is no need for alarm, Mr Easter, and I'll stop if you wish to get out.' The chauffeur had seen my actions in the driving-mirror and he opened the grille again. 'The doors are fitted with safety catches and you have to turn a little knob above the lock to release them. We have only a mile or two to go sir, but would you like me to draw up?'

'No, please drive on.' I turned the knob in question and found he had spoken the truth. No forcible abduction was taking place so I relaxed slightly and viewed the passing scene. For some reason, the streets of central London were decked with bunting and banners and floral decorations. Probably in honour of the absurd church conference. I hadn't heard that any royal wedding or similar jollification was in the offing.

The cigar was a Double Corona, the coffee tasted delicious after the prison fare and I had not been kidnapped. Some benevolent person, possibly a newspaper proprietor, had been told of my plight. He'd put up the bail and most probably would lay on a top-line Q.C. for my defence. A kindly gesture, but though I'd thank my benefactor, the Q.C. could wait. I had a few contacts in the London underworld who knew a darned sight more than any lawyers and, as it was over a week since Mr Brown had brought his wanderers home, there might be news of them. I was thinking who I'd talk to first when journey's end was reached. We turned under an arch and drew up before a building which was as impressive as the car itself. The chauffeur climbed out and opened the door for me with a salute.

'This is the gentleman our master is expecting, Mr Haselton.' He turned to a bit-part Negro actor from a low-budget film about the Old South, who had hurried out from the house. A respectful old darkie with a frock coat, grey-striped trousers and a bow tie that was as black as his face.

'Thank you, Martin.' Rastus dismissed the chauffeur and beamed at me. 'I am Haselton, the master's butler, sah, and it is my privilege to bid you welcome on his behalf.' The chauffeur's words and Haselton's garb had made the introduction unnecessary, but it's always nice to be made welcome, so I grinned back, said I was glad to make his acquaintance, and followed him up the steps to the house.

House! The place was a ruddy palace and my eyes boggled at its opulence. The entrance hall had oval walls faced with rose-pink marble and its curved marble staircase would have suited the King of Ruritania down to the ground. Chandeliers gleamed from the frescoed ceiling and the floor was a vast mosaic showing nymphs and shepherds disporting themselves in a forest. A bloody good mosaic, but the pictures on display were even more attractive and I halted to have a look at one of them. Three naked ladies, each as well-endowed as Peg, playing with a young lad who looked as though he'd be better employed kicking a football around. A Rubens, and a genuine one too. I was sure that my host wouldn't settle for reproductions.

'Please follow me, Mr Easter. We mustn't keep the master waiting.' The butler's tone was a model of deferential urgency, though I found the way he emphasized 'master' disturbing. Not as though he had referred to his employer or the owner of the house, but a much bigger pot. *The Master* — guess who?

But whoever the personage might be, I didn't want to irritate him by tardiness and I hurried obediently after his domestic.

'Mr William Easter is here, Master.' Well-trained servants do not knock and Haselton flung open a door and bowed ceremoniously. He made the announcement sound as though the prodigal son had returned to the fold and was ready for a good tuck-in after the swines' husks. I put on an ingratiating smile and stepped forward into a room which was only slightly smaller than the hall and just as opulent.

Two figures rose from a couch to welcome me. The first was Peggy and her presence was not really surprising. It would have been uncharitable for our benefactor to have bailed-out one partner of the union and left the other behind bars. But Peg's companion certainly surprised me. He was completely unexpected and for a moment I could only stammer and stare at him.

'You ... you ... what on earth are you doing here?'

15

'What am I doing, Bill? Need you, who know me so well, ask such a question?' Peggy's companion was Bishop Gerald Hurst-Hutchins and I didn't know him well — nobody did. His mind was too tortuous for a normal human being to fathom. He was a vast man — taller than myself, even stouter than Peg, and glittering robes and regalia made him even more impressive. His green silk cassock was trimmed with ermine, a gold cross studded with rubies dangled before his purple stole and his episcopal ring sported another ruby which was as large as a sparrow's egg. The whole get-up was topped by a white skull-cap sprinkled with green sequins, and I suspected that the sequins were emeralds. Bishop Gerry did himself proud.

'I am busy with God's work as always, Bill. Surely you don't doubt that?'

'Of course not, Bishop.' God's work was Hurst-Hutchins's meal-ticket and he had a hearty appetite. 'I'm merely surprised to see you in London. One would have thought that the new president of Leonia would have affairs of state to attend to.'

'Quite true, dear boy, but I am a churchman as well as a politician.' He held out his ring to be kissed, but I ignored the gesture and shook his hand. Hurst-Hutchins had put up bail for us, but he was still in my debt for past services and I wouldn't kowtow to him.

'His Lordship is here for the ecumenical conference,

darling.' Peggy simpered in admiration. They say that like attracts like and she had a crush on the fat brute. 'I read about his arrival in the paper and asked if I could telephone him. The Governor allowed me to if ... ' She stopped abruptly and I could guess what that *if* signified. In return for the telephone call, Peg had promised to give evidence against me should the need arise.

'In any case that's why we're free, Bill. As soon as I'd spoken to the bishop, he sent over the bail money and a car to fetch me to the embassy.'

'And welcome to the embassy, my friends.' There was a fine display of bottles on a lacquered table and his lordship mixed three gin fizzes — his favourite tipple. 'Our new embassy, of course. This property has only recently been purchased from the Chicago meat-millionairess, Mrs Sadie Klung; what delicious names some Americans have. We are rather camping out at the moment, I'm afraid, but I hope you are not too uncomfortable.

'Yes, Bill, I suppose that your surprise at my presence is natural enough. Leonia is in an even worse economic situation than usual and I am sorely needed at home.' The statement didn't surprise me in the least. Leonia has always been a poverty-stricken dump and buying up palaces and old masters wouldn't start any financial boom.

'But, as I'm sure you'll agree, humanity comes before nationality.' He paused and repeated the phrase sonorously. 'Humanity before Nationality. Rather a catchy slogan that. I think I might use it during my speech to the conference.

'Cheers, my dears.' We were each handed a frothing glass and he raised his own. 'World peace and Christian unity have always been very close to my heart and I felt that the Leonese people could spare me for such good causes.' Though his fat-circled eyes tried to look soulful, I could guess the reason for the bishop's visit to England. After Asmonda's death the Leonians had developed a taste for revolutions and another one might be in the offing. It would probably not succeed because Pal Gerry had an efficient secret-police force, but he had decided to make himself scarce till the plotters were under lock and key.

'You really do have a vivid imagination, Bill.' Like Mr Brown and Sally Lambert, Hurst-Hutchins was a bit of a mind-reader and he had rumbled my thoughts. 'Your suspicions are quite unfounded, however. Apart from the usual economic problems all is quiet in Leonia and I am here for the most worthy of motives; peace and money. Quite a tidy sum of money, as it happens.' He sat down and crossed his bolster-like legs.

'Church buildings are allowed to decay, clergy are poorly paid, but have you any idea how much the churches themselves are worth, Peggy?' He ogled her like a Victorian rake after a chorus-girl. She hadn't a clue, but I'd read about the Vatican treasures and I knew that the Church of England Commissioners are one of the world's richest business corporations, so I said they were rolling.

'Quite so, Bill. The gentlemen are wallowing in filthy lucre and the welfare of emergent African nations always appeals to their normally stony hearts. Strange how do-gooders have such a liking for blacks.' He sucked at his gin fizz through a straw. 'Be that as it may, I intend to profit from those do-gooders and that conference is the key to their bank.'

'What do a few Catholic cardinals, Anglican bishops

and such-like matter?' I had shrugged and Hurst-Hutchins nodded and handed me an ash-tray for my cigar. 'Exactly, Bill. They're not worth a tinker's cuss. But a bishop, who is also a political head of state, is quite a different kettle of fish and I am going to make a positive contribution to Christian unity. A theological college in Constitution where the faithful of all denominations may study God's word in harmony.'

'A college which will cost a packet, Bishop.' Judging by its weight the ash-tray was solid gold and I was suitably impressed. 'Enough to keep Leonia solvent and pay for little luxuries like this.'

'More than enough, my boy, and I have already been assured of half the necessary budget.' He smiled around the huge, ostentatious room. 'Cardinal Alberti, the papal legate, has promised a most generous contribution, my brothers at Canterbury and York are eager to assist and P.A.U.A. — that's Dr Maxwell, the President of the American Unitarian Association, is kindness personified.

Only the Moderator of the Church of Scotland, Professor MacSpey, and Archimandrite Kyprogorous are raising difficulties. A tight-fisted couple, but I have no doubt that MacSpey can be won over in time and Kyprogorous will find that it's a question of Greek meeting Greek. He's having an affair with a little Cypriot deacon and his flock would love to hear about their fun and games.' Though there was no physical resemblance between the two men, Hurst-Hutchins reminded me of the crafty Mr Brown.

'That should explain my presence in London, dear friends, and I'm all agog to hear about your tribulations. I naturally paid your bail for friendship's sake, but Peggy's brief account on the telephone whetted my appetite. As she only got here shortly before you, Bill, I want to know more.' He finished his drink and smirked at us.

'I gather that the police and the magistrates hardly believed a word you said, but I'm a credulous sort of chap, I love a good yarn, so try me.' Like hell he was credulous, the Reverend Gerry trusted nobody and if he was offered a Picasso for a fiver he'd have it examined by an expert before handing over one penny.

A hard case, the bishop. A hawk in the plumage of a great, swollen peacock and he hadn't provided our bail out of friendship or for the sake of an enthralling yarn. Peg had done more than whet his appetite and I realized something which had puzzled me since I entered the room. The bland, self-confident manner was a sham and the President of Leonia was worried stiff.

'John Brown — an unoriginal pseudonym. Queen Victoria's devoted coachman, or an American slavery abolitionist who originated a popular marching song. Also the character in a pre-war film one had to say *Yes* to.' We had started our account of the story and Hurst-Hutchins leaned back on the sofa with his eyes half-closed.

'Brown — a colour associated with Adolf Hitler, who was born at Braunau, founded the Brown Shirts, held his meetings at the Brown House and married Eva Braun. The colour of decay and just the kind of name the man might have adopted. Like Jack the Ripper, your Mr Brown has a perverse sense of fun.'

'You know him, Bishop?' I was sitting bolt upright in my chair. 'You know who Brown really is?'

'Possibly, Bill, because the world is my parish and I know a great many people.' He side-stepped the question and veered to a different topic; Brown's passengers.

'Seven men and two women who were brutally brainwashed in that camp and then given a variant of the Russian truth drug. A chemical which sealed the effects of the brainwashing and produced complete obedience.

'The result — zombies. Servile and apparently pious robots who hear heavenly voices and are as good as gold unless they are provoked.' He opened his eyes and smiled at Peggy. 'I'm sure you pack a heavy punch and the provocation was considerable, my dear.

'Zombies would be useful possessions in certain circumstances, wouldn't they?' He was speaking as much to himself as to us and the eyelids flickered shut again. 'I wonder what use our mutual acquaintance hopes to make of them.'

'You do know who Brown is, Bishop.' I felt like shaking him. 'You also know where he can be found, so why the hell can't you come into the open and tell us?'

'I have my reasons, Bill, and please do not swear at me, because you are very much in my debt and in my power. Though this house is foreign territory, there is nothing to stop me sending you back to the British authorities and reclaiming the bail money.' He sat up and helped himself to another drink, but did not offer us refills. 'I was informed that the man ... let's call him Brown for the time being ... was dead. That he and his adherents had been liquidated before the revolution. It now appears I was wrongly informed and my intelligence corps will be in for a reshuffle. Yes, heads will roll when I get back to Leonia. All the time, the man was in Galando tinkering up his yacht.

'But please continue with your story, Bill.' Apart from sucking noisily at his straw, he remained silent till I reached the part about the fire and then he stared hard at me. 'What is that? You honestly expect me to believe that he destroyed the girl?'

'There was no girl, Bishop.' Peggy answered him. 'Brown's note said that the owner of the ship was in his cabin, but it was a lie. As Bill just told you, the thing was only a wax dummy. It was *us* Brown wanted to destroy, though God knows why he tried to do it that way.'

'I can guess why, my dear.' Hurst-Hutchins nodded very slowly. 'Have you never heard of a Viking's funeral?'

Apparently Peggy hadn't because her expression remained blank, but I've had a sound education and I explained. When a Norse chieftain died, the body was placed in his long ship with slaves and other chattels to keep it company in the next world. The ship was then set alight and allowed to drift off towards the sunset and Valhalla. A wasteful, ostentatious display of wealth and I didn't see how it fitted the situation.

'Because that dummy, as you call it, could not perish alone.' Hurst-Hutchins seemed to be speaking in riddles. 'The girl had to have attendants on her long journey and you and Peggy were all that Hans could spare. His other passengers may have work to do.'

I didn't know what he was driving at, but two pieces of information had emerged. Brown's first name was Hans, which is the German form of John, and he was supposed to have been killed before the revolution. Did that mean he was one of Asmonda's agents as I'd first thought?

'Good heavens no, Bill.' Hurst-Hutchins heaved himself up from the sofa. 'The girl was the only person Hans served and the fact that he burned her and changed the yacht's name to *Pandora* offers some very disturbing possibilities.' He crossed to a window and stared out at the embassy grounds. The weather had started to clear at last and it would not be long before divers went down to the yacht. '*Pandora*, the woman who released evil on the earth. When you were in Leonia you must have heard of the Cult of the Virgin, Bill.'

'Of course I don't mean the Virgin Mary.' He turned with a frown at my answer. 'I mean the White Virgin of Maniporo and how did the prophecy go?' He paused for a second and then quoted aloud. ' "After the saint returns to her place in heaven, the mockers will weep."

'She has returned, it seems, and I was one of those mockers.' There was a greyish tinge on Hurst-Hutchins's normally florid face. 'I mocked that silver woman and I wonder — just wonder.' He gave a slight shudder and walked towards us.

'Bill — Peggy, we're old friends and you're not lying to me are you — not trying to frighten me? There really was a wax figure in the cabin? You saw it with your own eyes?'

'I did more than see it.' His disbelief irritated me and I raised my voice. 'I carried the thing out on deck and it damn near cost me my life.'

'Of course you did, my boy, and I don't doubt your word. It's just that you've made me rather anxious.' *Rather* anxious. The grey tinge was off-white now and his face resembled a vast lump of suet.

'Mr Bloody John Brown, as he calls himself, and his bloody brainwashed puppets must be located and dealt with quickly; bloody quickly.' Three bloodies from a beneficed clergyman — and a bishop to boot — were a bit much, but I shared his sentiments to the full and said I'd be only too happy to do the dealing with Brown if I could find him.

'Good chap. Good, loyal, dependable, old Bill. I can always rely on you in a tight corner.' The hand that squeezed my arm was oozing with sweat and it left a damp patch on my jacket. 'We'll cook the fellow's goose all right. We'll run him to earth and settle his hash; just as we settled Asmonda's.

'We must do, because if we fail, something terrible could happen. I suspect that the man may be planning a crime so cruel and senseless that my mind boggles at the very thought of it.'

I tried to imagine what his mind-boggling act might be. Letting off an atom bomb — dumping plague bacillus in a reservoir. There were too many possibilities to consider, so I asked him what he thought Brown was up to.

'Something terrible, as I have said, Bill. An insane and wanton crime which will go down in history as the epitome of human wickedness. I honestly believe that among other things, the man may intend ... ' The bishop paused and repeated himself to stress the gravity of the situation. 'May intend to kill — *Me.*'

16

An unoriginal choice of victim. A lot of people must have wanted to kill Hurst-Hutchins and the news that Brown had it in for him did not surprise me. Though I was interested to know for what reason, and how, the assassination would be attempted. I had to wait a long time for the answers.

'Damnation! I said we were not to be disturbed.' A telephone on his desk was ringing and the bishop picked it up petulantly. 'Miss Smithers, your memory is really atrocious and I told you that I was accepting no calls.

'Who, do you say? Oh, that's quite a different matter. If Canterbury himself is on the line, I will naturally speak to him.' Worry and petulance changed to a girlish simper as his secretary put through the caller.

'Good afternoon, Your Grace. How lovely to hear from you and I trust you are enjoying the best of health and spirits.'

'Yes, I am as well as can be expected, thank you, Your Grace, though my responsibilities to church and state are heavy burdens to bear.'

'What — what is that?' The simper was a trifle less pronounced. 'You are worried about the college scheme? Before ratifying our arrangements, you and His Eminence, Cardinal Alberti, consider that there should be inquiries into Leonia's internal affairs? A fact-finding commission composed of British parliamentarians and members of the Society of Jesus?' There was a long pause, Hurst-Hutchins's pallor vanished and his face became brick red.

'I'm afraid I certainly cannot agree to the proposal, Your Grace. In the first place, both M.P.s and Jesuits are born trouble-makers and renowned for mendacity and subterfuge; justly renowned. Secondly, I am Leonia's legally elected president and such a commission would be a slur on my personal honour. May I ask, Your Grace, who prompted this outrageous suggestion when the college contract was virtually agreed?'

Mendacity — subterfuge — personal honour — blah-blah-blah, I thought while he listened to his superior. Hurst-Hutchins was a fine one to talk.

'Aha-ha, so that's it. You received a report from Canon Chivers of the Anglican mission at Bolonka. That explains everything, and I can put your mind at rest here and now. Chivers is mentally unbalanced and he bears a grudge against me because I refused to elevate him to the rank of rural dean. Your Grace will appreciate how deranged the man is when I tell you that he was expelled from the British Communist party for Trotskyite sympathies.' Hurst-Hutchins's expression showed that Canon Chivers would also be expelled from Leonia in the near future.

'You say that you have been supplied with photographs and documentary evidence. Signed statements proving corruption in the police and the taxation departments which are under my personal control. Lies and forgeries, my dear Archbishop. Complete and utter poppycock.' He snapped his fingers to register contempt, but it was a soft, flabby snap and I doubted whether *Canterbury* heard him.

'Pictures of chained convicts working on the roads? Men and women flogged for trivial offences? Orphan girls forcibly conscripted into state brothels? Preposterous charges and there's a simple answer to the last three. The late President Asmonda did tolerate such abominations, may God forgive him, and the photographs were obviously taken during his regime. As for the accusations of corruption, you know me too well to credit anything of that sort.

'I see.' He sat down on a stool beside the telephone and sighed. 'If that is your final word, sir, I must ask for a moment to consider the situation.' His face was still angry and then a thought seemed to strike him and a sly grin crinkled his sagging jowls. 'Very well, Your Grace, a commission there shall be. But I am sure you will agree that it should not leave for Leonia till I have returned there after the conference.' On the surface, an abject retreat, but I knew that Gerry hadn't surrendered. As de Gaulle said after hooking it from the krauts, 'We have lost a battle, not a war.'

'Thank you, Archbishop. The success of that conference is my main ambition at the moment and I know you share my view that humanity comes before nationality.' He delivered the slogan gushingly.

'Yes, of course we can discuss your wishes after the service at Westminster Abbey tonight and how I am looking forward to that service. I understand that all the delegates intend to be present so let us hope and pray it will be our first stepping-stone towards harmony.

'Till this evening then, Your Grace.' He replaced the telephone on its rest and glowered. 'Bastard! The stupid, credulous old bastard accepts the word of a dotty parish priest in a back-woods mission and rejects mine. How despicable can a man become?' The bishop's injured innocence was a treat to watch, but though the charges were probably true, I sympathized with him. His administration was harsh. It had to be, because his subjects were used to Asmonda's iron rod and any relaxation would be regarded as a sign of weakness. Roads must be made, and if the convicts were not fettered they'd run into the jungle and resort to brigandage. The petty malefactors would much prefer a taste of the cat to a term in prison, and the orphan girls were far better off in medically inspected state brothels. Left on their own they'd either starve or spread disease on the streets.

All the same, Hurst-Hutchins was on a poor wicket because the corruption charges could be easily proved, and then God help him. Goodbye to the thumping loan for a college, which he probably never intended to build. Goodbye to his bishopric; the Church Commissioners are sharp businessmen, but they draw the line at extortion. Also, goodbye to his life if Mr Brown had it in for him, so I asked what he intended to do on that score.

'Protect myself, Bill, and I have formidable defences.' He clicked his tongue and another sound followed. A tail like a rhinoceros-hide whip thumped against the floor and the owner of the tail emerged from a corner of the room. An animal — an enormous and repulsive animal. The twin sister of the hound of the Baskervilles which cocked an evil eye at Peggy and me and then sidled across to Hurst-Hutchins.

'This is Hecate, one of the embassy's most trusty employees and already completely devoted to myself.' He stroked the great, brindled muzzle nuzzling his shoulder. 'Take a basis of a Great Dane for size, add Bull Mastiff for strength, Alsatian for obedience and savour with a pinch of Dobermann Pincher for savagery. Sorry about the pun but I do adore them so; and what have you got? Hecate, a lethal weapon whose one aim in life is to serve Daddy. Isn't that true, my little darling?'

He fondled one of the little darling's battle-scarred ears.

'Dogs know their friends and they also know their friends' enemies, don't they, Sweetie-Pie? If I were to say A-T-T-A-C-K, Bill, she'd tear you both to ribbons.' I was glad that he'd spelled out the words, because the boast was obviously true. The brute might love Daddy, but she didn't care for Peggy or myself and her hackles rose as she looked at us.

'I don't think I need to worry too much about Mr Brown, Bill, but I'd like to know what you'd do if you knew where to find him.' Not an easy question. What I would like to do was to beat the daylights out of him, but Brown also had devoted defenders and I was in enough trouble already. As Dodd had pointed out, high treason is one of the three crimes still punishable by the death penalty, the others being certain forms of mutiny and setting fire to a naval dockyard; so I told Hurst-Hutchins that I'd tip off the cops and collect the reward money.

'Quite so. A public-spirited aim, even though it is mainly motivated by greed. You've always been a greedy chap, and it's a bad failing ... the root of all evil.' His desk supported an intercom as well as the telephone and he pressed a button and jabbered something in an African dialect which was meaningless to me.

'Yes, a bad fault is avarice, and as a Christian prelate it is my bounden duty to help you conquer it.' He had switched off the set and pivoted round on the stool. 'Maybe a period of quiet meditation might help. Peace and tranquillity in which your mind can dwell on more spiritual matters, and here are Sergeant N'gomo and Private Windibanks who will see that you are kept quiet.

'Tweedledee and Tweedledum, as I call them.' He

grinned at the two men who came into the room, but they didn't grin back. The poor dears lacked a sense of humour and they were unfamiliar with the works of Lewis Carroll. Two hulking, jet-black embassy guards and as like as two peas. They both wore identical grey suits, they were both built like weight-lifters and they both had wooden, expressionless faces. They also sported identical .45 calibre revolvers of Japanese manufacture and both revolvers were out of their holsters.

One gun pointed at me and one at Peggy. The dog snarled, the Lord Bishop tittered.

17

I'd always imagined that nothing Gerry Hurst-Hutchins said or did would ever surprise me, but his sudden change of attitude was astonishing in the extreme. Before the telephone call from *Canterbury*, he'd been eager for our help against Mr Brown, who might be plotting to kill him. Then, just a few minutes after the call, he'd summoned his two stalwarts and we were led away to the cells at pistol-point. I couldn't have been more flabbergasted if I'd received a shock from an electric appliance which was not connected to the mains.

I was also bloody angry, because I don't like cells and I'd had a basinful of them recently. Though our quarters were a damn sight better than the prison. We had a large bed-sitting-room with an adjoining bathroom, a radio set and a drinks cabinet to keep us amused and there were flowers on the dressing-table. A comfortable place of confinement, but a cell just the same. The windows were barred, the door had a spy-hole as well as a lock, and Sergeant N'gomo was stationed outside. I could see his ugly black pan constantly eyeing us through the glass. Only one security item appeared to be lacking. The radio's presence suggested that the suite was not bugged and bugging would have done our captors little good if it had been. I'd turned the set on to its full volume and you can't hear a close conversation against a blast of pop music.

'I know what he's up to, Bill. I've suddenly realized why we're locked in here.' About half an hour had passed and Peggy whispered angrily in my ear. 'It's all your fault. You shouldn't have told the bishop we were hoping to claim the reward money because that's what he's after.'

Though Peg's anger was unjust, and I didn't like her moist breath spraying my face, I warmed towards her slightly because she had probably guessed the truth. Hurst-Hutchins had intended to con his fellow clerics over the college and their proposed inquiry might expose him. No lolly would be forthcoming from Rome or Canterbury or wherever the head of the Unitarians hangs out, and he needed lolly. He needed it badly and I'd shown him another possible source of supply. The rewards for Mr Brown's passengers — my rewards. Not a large amount by Gerry's standards, but enough to tide him over till more fund-raising schemes presented themselves.

One says that life can be unfair at times, but it's usually people who cause the unfairness. The police hadn't listened to Peggy or myself, but they'd give the president of a friendly power their full attention. Hurst-Hutchins obviously knew Brown's real name and he might have a clue where he was hiding out. If he could locate that hiding-place and tip off the authorities, he'd reap the rewards, and we were to be kept at the embassy till that happy event occurred.

Unless we could get to Brown first we would be in for a spell on National Assistance, so the problem of escape was all-important. I stared around the room for about the twentieth time and realized that escaping posed quite a problem. Windows with bars, a locked door and a man with a gun watching us through a peep-hole.

Or was he watching *us*? I looked at the tiny glass panel and moved away from Peggy. The good sergeant had small interest in me. His eyes were riveted on Peg and, as usual, hope sprang eternal to the human breast. I'd heard that Negroes are often attracted by fat white women and friend N'gomo was no exception. He fancied Peggy — he thought she was a real dish — and if his carnal desire was stronger than the call of duty, we might be able to profit from it. I thought of Joseph and Potiphar's wife again, but the cases were different. Joseph was an intelligent, pure-minded youth, who laid off out of respect for his god and his master. Our jailor was a lascivious half-wit and his god was probably an idol. A heathen who bowed down to wood and stone. Nor was Peggy Hurst-Hutchins's wife, so he need have no qualms about cuckolding the master.

I took another squint at the peep-hole and saw open lust in the staring eyes. If Peggy had that effect on him while wearing a respectably tailored uniform, what couldn't she do by showing a bit of leg, as the vulgar say? I crossed back to her and started to explain my plan, but I only needed to say a few words. Peg had also noticed N'gomo's amorous gaze — she caught on immediately and switched off the radio.

'You look tired, Bill, so why not have a bath?' She raised her voice in the hope that our guardian could hear her. 'We might as well make ourselves comfortable, even though we're prisoners. Helpless captives and completely in the sergeant's power.' However thick the door might be, N'gomo must have heard her last sentence because it was bellowed out like a foghorn in a gale. 'Go and have a good soak and be as long as you like. I'll follow you when you're finished.'

'I think I will, Peggy.' She was ready to do her stuff and I had to prepare for mine, so I nipped into the bathroom, leaving the door slightly ajar, and turned on the taps. My main requirement was a weapon, because, by and large, the black races are stronger and more agile than the whites, as their superiority in athletics and boxing proves. The average Negro is more than a match for a European of similar size and condition and Sergeant N'gomo was bigger than I am ... far bigger, and he looked in far better training. He was also provided with a revolver and, though Peg's a useful partner in a rough house, I had to even the odds.

A weapon was available. The low-level lavatory flush tank had a removable porcelain top. Heavy and hard and durable, and just the thing to crack a skull. I removed it and returned to the door, peering out through the gap between the frame.

Peggy's striptease was in progress. A spectacle which I'd witnessed before and found extremely boring, even though she had worn more exotic underwear on the previous occasions. She was removing her jacket and blouse to reveal a drab, khaki-coloured bra, which had presumably been supplied to her by the prison authorities, and proceeded to unzip her skirt, leering towards the peep-hole with what she imagined was girlish allure.

It didn't allure me. She looked damn silly and my hopes began to fade. N'gomo might be a bone-head with a crush on porkers, but the performance was just too corny. His thoughts of love must have vanished and duty and self-preservation returned.

I was wrong, and duty had gone to the winds. Peg's skirt lay on the floor, a pair of prison-issue knickers were visible and soon she would have company. I heard the key turn in the lock and saw the door start to open. The bait had been taken and our jailor was yielding to temptation.

'Here I come, my fat, white pigeon.' Lover Boy used almost the same form of address as the Lascar stoker who had pestered Peggy in Sydney, but he did not claim his reward then and there. The bastard was crafty as well as lecherous and he wasn't going to have me interrupting the orgy. He tiptoed across the carpet with the heavy pistol looking like a kid's toy in his huge hand, though he didn't intend to kill me unless Hurst-Hutchins gave the order. At least I hoped he didn't. My guess was he planned to ram the pistol under the bathroom door as a wedge to keep me out of harm's way. If that happened our scheme would come to nought and Peg suffer a fate worse than death.

'Don't you want me, Sergeant?' I needn't have worried on Peggy's account. She was right on the ball, and she stepped in front of him and ripped off her bra with a single powerful jerk. 'I certainly want you, darling. I saw you watching me through the window and I know we're after the same thing.' She nodded towards the bathroom. 'Don't worry about him. He always goes to sleep in a hot bath, so take me, Big Man. Take me now.

'I said *now*, Sergeant N'gomo.' He was staring hypnotized and paralysed by the vast expanse of mammalian flesh and Peggy flung her arms round his waist and swung him round so that his back was towards me. A huge back — a giant's back, rippling with muscle under his tight jacket, and the giant had to be felled with one blow before he could shout for help. I raised the lavatory top with both hands, kicked open the door and let him have it on the skull as though I was driving home the last spike of the last length of the first transcontinental railroad.

I'd said that N'gomo was a bonehead and I was right. It felt as though I'd hit a boulder and I was wrong in thinking that porcelain is a durable material. It shattered on impact and I was left holding a portion of the rim when he swung round and looked at me. He appeared dazed by the blow but not stunned and I clenched my fists and prepared for a battle I was bound to lose. The sergeant had an ally and the sounds of our punch-up would bring Private Windibanks to the rescue.

But I, also, had an ally and she acted promptly. A shoe had been slipped off and Peg slammed it home on the exact spot where the porcelain had connected. I heard a crack of bone, saw N'gomo's eyes close and his mouth drop open, and watched him topple slowly to the floor. He was out cold and our first barrier had been removed.

I picked up the revolver and waited for Peggy to make herself decent.

Our prison was on the third storey, but we reached the staircase unnoticed and I led the way down with N'gomo's pistol at the ready and the safety-catch off. I intended to use that gun without mercy if the need arose. Hurst-Hutchins didn't want to kill us, but he wanted to keep us in mothballs till the rewards had been claimed. He must have told his staff to shoot if we tried to escape and our deaths wouldn't worry him. The bodies could either be buried in the embassy grounds or shipped off to Leonia with diplomatic baggage.

We had reached the second floor and the coast remained clear. Though the president's own quarters were opulent in the extreme, much of the house seemed empty and unfurnished. Probably most of the staff were still roughing it at the old building.

The first floor. I halted at the sound of approaching footsteps and slid the revolver inside my coat. Only a female serf lugging along a vacuum cleaner and she passed us with a respectful nod and

'Afternoon, sir and madam.'

The ground floor — the big, marble-walled hall and the way to freedom lay ahead. My spirits soared as we hurried towards the door and then they plunged like falling rocks, because the exit was blocked. Human ears had not noted our departure, but other ears were keener. A huge brown-and-grey shape had emerged from Hurst-Hutchins's study and was stationed in front of us with teeth bared and hackles up. Hecate, the *little darling*, ready to spring if we moved a muscle. A formidable guardian and, if I missed with the first bullet, the brute's teeth would be in my throat. I was quite liable to miss too, because the blow I'd given N'gomo had left my hands shaky. I stopped obediently and resorted to cunning.

'Lord Bishop — sah. Please come quickly, Massa. Trouble, sah, heap bad trouble.' I don't claim that the imitation was perfect, but it must have resembled N'gomo's voice and the ruse worked.

'What trouble, Sergeant?' Hurst-Hutchins had appeared in the doorway with an irritated frown which vanished abruptly when he saw us. 'You, Bill ... You and Peggy.'

'Yes, Gerald dear,' I said, mimicking his own speech. 'The visitors are back.' A quick moving dog is a difficult target, but I could drill the bishop with my eyes closed and he knew it.

'Tell that animal to return to the corner where it belongs, and then we'll all have another pally-wally natter about a lot of things.' I grinned as he gave Hecate the necessary orders and my pleasure increased while he lead the way into his sanctum and I closed the door behind us. The whip was in my hand and I was going to enjoy plying it.

18

'Very well, Bill. I admit that I double-crossed you and dear Peggy, but it was partly in your own interest and my motives were quite unselfish.' Hurst-Hutchins cowered before the revolver. 'The man you and Peggy know as Brown is dangerous — horribly dangerous — and I didn't want you to risk your lives.' The first part of the statement was quite unnecessary. Brown had already tried to burn us to death and damn nearly succeeded.

'Why should you have to tackle him when I have plenty of professionals available?' I had to smile at that. Sergeant N'gomo was one of those professionals and all he'd be tackling for a while was a diet of rusks and beef tea, or whatever they give to patients with fractured skulls.

'I also admit that I hoped to claim part of the reward for those criminals he is sheltering, but not for myself — oh no.' He emphasized the *No* emotionally. 'Leonia is such a poor, backward country and many of my people subsist at starvation level. I was relying on the college funds to bolster our economy and after that senile beast at Canterbury went back on his word and demanded an inquiry I was heartbroken. The reward monies seemed like a gift of God, Bill.'

'A gift to compensate for the other gifts you have bought yourself.' I looked around the huge, luxurious room and picked up the gold ash-tray with my free hand. 'The injured nobility act does not suit you, Bishop, so cut it out and sit down.

'No, not behind the desk.' I nodded to a chair by the wall. 'Over there beside the door where I can cover you and any interfering visitors who may appear. That's better, and now for our talk, or rather your talk. You obviously know a great deal about Mr Brown, so who is he and where can we find him?'

'I can't answer the second question, Bill, and please put that thing away. I do hate having guns pointed at me.' So does every sane person, but he'd ordered his retainers to point a couple of them at us not long ago and the muzzle stayed trained on his belly.

'As to Brown's true identity' — He squirmed uneasily on the chair as I laid aside the ash-tray. 'From what you have told me it seems that the man may be Hans Braune who kept the shrine of the Girl.' Our faces remained blank and the bishop repeated himself. 'The Girl ... the White Virgin of Maniporo and she was the one person Soji Asmonda really feared.'

The original shrine was near a pool outside the village of Maniporo, some hundred miles upriver from Constitution, where an early Portuguese missionary was said to have baptized his converts before suffering martyrdom. The Keeper of the Shrine was an elderly woman who later became known as the Girl.

'She was a European, Bill, but I never saw her alive and I have no idea where she came from or what her real name was. The natives referred to her as *Sarkini Kal*, which means The Old Healer in their language, or *Sissie Mega* in Leonese-English patois, though God knows why.' If God knew, I was certain Hurst-Hutchins also knew, but though he was lying, I didn't interrupt him. The woman was of no interest to me. I wanted to hear about Mr Brown.

'As far as I could gather, the lady had settled in Leonia a long time ago — probably during the First World War — and taken up residence in Maniporo. She was a regular attendant at the shrine and, after a while, the cult became centred around her, as she was considered to have powers of prophecy and healing. Water from the pool accompanied by her blessing was said to cure indigestion, impotence and sterility and other ailments, and doubtless it did. So much illness stems from here and responds to psycho-suggestion.' He tapped his forehead with a sausage-like finger.

'The years went by, a monastery was built, pilgrims flocked there for treatment and a glimpse into the future, and Madam was regarded as a sort of "She who *must* be Obeyed".' How I loved that Rider Haggard story when I was a boy. I suppose I must have a masochistic streak, because it gave me the most delicious fantasies.

'However, as more years flitted past and the poor dear grew old, her spiritual powers declined with her physical attractions. As you may know, Negroes have a penchant for young white women, but being blessed by a crone was hardly exciting.' I did know about that penchant for white women and not only young ones. N'gomo's disgusting exhibition over Peg proved that the age group was flexible.

'By the time Hans Braune came on the scene, the cult was well on the decline, but before I tell you about Braune, please — please — stop pointing that gun at me, Bill. It might go off accidentally and I just can't concentrate.' He was staring at the revolver like a rabbit hypnotized by a stoat, so I lowered the muzzle and let him continue.

Braune had settled in Leonia a year or two before Hurst-Hutchins's arrival and he was very much a mystery man. Some people considered that he was a Nazi war-criminal on the run, some an unfrocked priest, others a doctor who'd been struck off. Any of the theories could be correct and certainly he had some medical knowledge and was fascinated by religion. Whatever the truth about his past, his destination was Maniporo and shortly after he reached the monastery a miracle was performed.

'A miracle as I said, my dear.' With the gun turned away from him Hurst-Hutchins was more relaxed and he grinned at Peggy's obvious disbelief. 'Sarkini Kal, the Old Healer, died but she rose from the dead. Her spirit was resurrected in the body of a young woman and the Girl of Maniporo was born.

'Naturally, the story was credited, Bill, and I don't have to tell you how gullible the Leonians are. They believed Asmonda's claim to be an immortal deity and they'll swallow anything.' True enough. Most of the dolts also believed that their present ruler was a benevolent father-figure slaving away in their interest.

'In a matter of weeks, pilgrims started to flock to the monastery again; monks and nuns were enrolled and Hans Braune was elevated to the rank of abbot on the Girl's instructions. The Guardian of the Holy One was the title she gave him and the Holy One herself laid on more miracles. The usual auto-suggestion cures as before, but there were others which did not stem from the brain.' Hurst-Hutchins's forehead received another tap. 'The girl could kill as well as cure, you see.

'She was on show to the more important pilgrims;

chiefs, government officials and so forth, and as their questions were answered skilfully and there was a strangely inhuman aura about her, the majority were impressed. Those she did not impress came to rather sticky ends and two of Soji Asmonda's magistrates died of internal haemorrhages after they got back to Constitution.

'The implications of black magic put the wind up poor, dear Soji, I can tell you, and he rushed off to Maniporo to pay his respects. On his return, it was clear that he'd swallowed Braune's claims hook, line and sinker and believed that the Girl was a goddess who could make or break him. That's how Braune got hold of the yacht. It belonged to Soji and he loaned it to him to ship pilgrims up the river.' The bishop grinned mirthlessly. 'I'm afraid you'd have been poorly rewarded if you sailed her to Constitution, Bill. After the revolution, all Soji's property was confiscated by the state. If she was still afloat, the *Pandora*, or *Matabele* to use the original name, would be my property now.

'After seeing the impression Soji had received, I decided to make a personal pilgrimage. My reasons were partly curiosity and partly anxiety. Soji Asmonda and I were real buddies in those days and the man was terrified of the Girl's powers. If there was a threat to his safety, it was my bounden duty as a friend and a Christian to look into it.'

Buddies — friend — bounden duty, I thought. Gerald Iscariot had been Asmonda's main threat and while greasing up to the president he was already planning to have him killed.

'I didn't go to Maniporo alone, of course, that would have been most rash.' Hurst-Hutchins smiled again. 'The senior members of my Church Lads' Brigade were due for a spell under canvas and I took along three dozen of them; great hulking fellows in their late teens, and all armed with sporting rifles. Muscular Christians to a man and devoted to myself. When we got to Maniporo, they pitched their tents outside the village and I told 'em to take appropriate action if I didn't return within an agreed time-limit. I also told them to show their guns to the villagers and make it clear that they meant business.

'What puzzled me on arrival at the monastery itself was the demeanour of the monks and nuns who were knocking around. They were all young and they all appeared to be odd in one way or another. Some seemed to be completely withdrawn and silent, as though they were in a state of trance, others almost frenzied with excitement. A few shuffled about like sick, mindless animals.

'Yes, Bill, it all tallied with what you told me about those people on the yacht and I began to wonder if Hans Braune might have been feeding 'em dope. The Girl's adherents certainly looked as though they were drugged and those I spoke to referred to her as a god. I felt pretty certain that they would lay down their lives if she ordered it, and take other lives if she gave the word. I was also pretty certain that the word must have been given already and I thought about Soji's two magistrates. One is liable to die with a dose of poison in one's guts.

'But talking is such thirsty work, my friends.' He looked longingly at the drinks table. 'Could we all have a fizzy-wizzy before I go on?' He could, but Peggy and I couldn't because we had to keep our heads clear. Peg mixed him a gin fizz and he took a long pull at the straw and continued.

'Braune himself answered your description of Mr Brown. A short, bearded man in his early sixties with a booming laugh, a constantly smiling mouth and the hardest eyes I'd ever seen. He greeted me pleasantly enough because he knew I had the confidence of Soji Asmonda, but I didn't think he was very pleased to see me: not at first.

'I'd better answer that, Bill.' The intercom on his desk had started to whirr. 'If I don't, my secretary will be worried and come to investigate.'

'Very well, but don't do anything foolish, like screaming for help.' I followed him to the desk and kept the pistol against his back throughout the conversation.

'Excuse me, Bishop, but if you have changed your mind about not going to Westminster Abbey, it is time for your Lordship to robe.' The woman's advice seemed unnecessary because His Lordship was already got up like the Archangel Gabriel. 'As you know, the service is due to start at seven.'

'Of course I know that, Miss Smithers, but I have not changed my mind, though I very much wish I could.' He looked at the clock: it was quarter to six. 'Such a shame, but I must be fit for the conference itself and the Abbey is always so chilly. Though my indisposition is mild at the moment, it could turn into a nasty bout of gastric flu if I don't take care of myself.' He belched and wheezed to demonstrate his sickness.

'Yes, I have aspirin and all I require, thank you, so just telephone the dean and make the necessary apologies for me.' Missing the service did not seem to distress him unduly and, as far as I could see, he was in fair physical health — if a man who weighs twenty-five stone and eats and drinks more than three normal people can ever be healthy. 'Make the apologies really profuse, Miss Smithers, and when Swarmi phones, put him straight through to me. I'm not available to anyone else.

'Let's go on with the story then.' He had switched off the set and returned to his seat by the wall. 'We'll discuss Braune in a moment, but I'd like to describe the trappings of religion he'd laid on first because they were good showmanship — the best.'

The monastery church had been got up like a fairground with coloured lights and statues everywhere. There was one of those organs that can produce the full range of an orchestra and two choirs were chanting away in a fog of incense. All the pomp and circumstance to impress simple souls, but the bishop lacked simplicity and it did not impress him.

'The crypt was impressive though.' Hurst-Hutchins's eyes lost their cynicism as he described the journey down to the inner sanctum. A long, steep staircase, lit by oil lamps. A long, winding corridor with monks stationed against the walls like sentinels. Braune bowing before a curtain and then drawing it aside and ushering his guest into the Holy of Holies.

'The girl herself also impressed me, Bill. She was reclining on a couch in semi-darkness, and though the lighting was dim she seemed to glow with a personal light which was both vital and ghostly, as Soji Asmonda had said. I could see her breast moving and when she started to answer my questions her voice sounded completely lifelike.'

'But *She* didn't answer them, Bishop.' I remembered how lifelike the figure on the yacht had appeared. 'Braune answered you.'

'Exactly, Bill, and what a story-spoiler you are.' He looked aggrieved, like a man who'd been interrupted just before the punch-line of a dirty joke. 'Braune was a ventriloquist and the Girl was a dummy, fitted with an electric bellows to give the impression of life. But not an ordinary dummy, Bill, no mere mechanical toy, Peggy; he explained that to me later. The wax was just a skin, a covering, and beneath it lay the actual body of *Sarkini Kal*. The Old Healer had died shortly after Braune's arrival at Maniporo and her corpse formed the base of his deception. Hans Braune was a confidence trickster, but he'd carried the con-trick too far and that was to be his undoing.'

'How, Bishop?' He had paused and was staring at the clock and Peggy prompted him. 'How had he gone too far?'

'He'd gone to the bitter end, my dear, and one can have too much of a good thing.' Hurst-Hutchins still kept his eyes on the clock as though its hurrying second-hand fascinated him. 'I'm certain I gave no physical sign that I'd spotted the deception, but as you know Brown-Braune is a bit of a mind-reader and he'd read my mind like a book. He had also realized that I'd be a useful ally and, when we returned from the crypt, he took me to his private quarters and laid the cards on the table. All fifty-six of 'em — the whole crooked pack.' His lips curled into a smile.

'One of the biggest swindles in history had been planned and I was offered a share in the proceeds. If an Anglican priest of high standing would bow down to Braune's Girl, the cult would snowball.

'And snowball not just in Leonia. Superstition is an African failing and, with professional stage-managership and the yacht to bring in pilgrims from other emergent nations, the good seed couldn't help sprouting. Braune believed that before twelve months had passed, half the continent would be in our pockets.

'Of course, I accepted the offer, Peggy.' Her question seemed to surprise him. 'It was an extremely attractive one and I fancied the ruse would work. Also, I had no choice. Braune knew that my Church Lads' Brigade were on the ball, he couldn't risk killing me at the monastery, but I had to think of the future. I didn't want one of the Girl's devotees coming to Constitution to pop poison into my grub.' He finished his drink, the straw making the usual squelching sound as it sucked up the dregs.

'I gave Hans Braune my solemn word of honour that I would collaborate with him, and the funny thing is that at the time I fully intended to keep my promise. But then, as soon as I got back to Constitution, I told Soji Asmonda exactly what was in the offing and added that Braune intended to kill him, which was obviously true. Soji claimed to be divine and Leonia could hardly support two deities.' He giggled loudly and though I couldn't find anything amusing in the barefaced betrayal, it explained why Brown might have it in for him.

'Soji was naturally extremely perturbed and annoyed at the deception and he acted with commendable promptitude. Units of his secret police were rushed to Maniporo and every living soul in the monastery was wiped out with machine-guns and flame-throwers. We imagined the matter was finished, but apparently we were wrong and Braune escaped taking the image with him. In any case, that's all I know and I think you can bring the rest of the story up to date, my friends.'

He was partly correct, but three vital points perplexed me. Mr Brown — I still couldn't think of him as Braune — had lost his disciples, the followers of the Girl who would sacrifice their lives for her if need be. He had escaped from the monastery and later learned that replacement acolytes were available. Bruno Kremer and his fellow prisoners, already partially brainwashed and pliable clay for the potter's hand. Brown had returned to Leonia, bribed the camp commandant to help him and taken his heavily sedated replacements to the *Pandora* which had been moved across the river to Galando.

That all fitted, but the puzzle was far from solved. Why had Brown destroyed the image of the Girl, using Peggy and me as burnt offerings for her Viking's funeral? What use did he intend to make of his loopy passengers in Europe? Finally, why had Hurst-Hutchins gone back on his word when he'd had so much to gain and fancied that the odds were favourable? Bishop Gerry loved power and if the ploy had worked, he and Brown would have ended up controlling as much territory as the Roman Empire.

'A fair question, but difficult to answer, Bill.' I had put it to him and he considered before replying. 'My faith in the enterprise vanished and anxiety took its place. I first imagined that Hans Braune was just a confidence trickster. A clever, cynical fellow after my own heart.' I wasn't sure that the bishop had a heart in the emotional sense, but I shared his opinion about Brown's cynicism and nodded.

'How wrong I was.' His eyes moved back to the clock and I sensed that important news was expected. 'Hans and I drank a toast to our partnership and then he took me down to the crypt again and we looked at the figure on the couch.

'I complimented him on the image, because it really was a beautiful piece of work, and he said he'd once studied art in London and it was in London that he'd first heard about the Maniporo shrine.

'No, he didn't tell me which art school he'd attended, Bill, and I'm afraid I didn't ask him.' The bishop shook his head vigorously — too vigorously — and I was sure he was lying again.

'But this is what made me decide to dissolve our partnership. As we looked down at the couch, I heard a sob and I turned and saw that Hans Braune was weeping. Tears were trickling from his little, hard eyes on to the bearded cheeks and I started to ask myself a question.

'Why? Why bother to treat a dead body with wax when it would have been so much easier to build a frame from wood or metal or plastic? Another difficult question, but those weeping eyes provided the answer. The fellow was no ordinary con-man. He believed that that thing — that dummy of dead flesh and dry bone and painted wax — really did have magical properties. That the Healer's spirit as well as her corpse was contained within the coating.

'Hans Braune was a religious maniac — a bent saint, and I don't dig bent saints, Bill.' The teenage jargon was unseemly on the lips of a middle-aged prelate, but the sentiment was sound enough. 'I don't dig saints of any description. They frighten me and I don't dig them at all.'

19

'Wait a moment, Bishop.' The telephone had started to ring and I could see that Hurst-Hutchins was nervous about answering it. He was eager for information, but he didn't want to share that information with me. I was also pretty sure that the call concerned Brown and I tried to imagine what I'd have done if I'd been in Gerry's shoes. He knew that Brown had landed in England and he knew that he'd once studied art in London. London is a large city, but there couldn't be all that many art schools knocking about, and the Leonian embassies, old and new, had plenty of minions to do the master's bidding. A little mingling in artistic clubs and public houses, a visit or two to the galleries might have led them to some of Brown's former acquaintances. My guess was that success had crowned their efforts and the caller was about to deliver glad tidings. I told Hurst-Hutchins exactly what he had to do and we walked across to the table.

'The President of Leonia here.' He picked up the receiver and obediently held it an inch or two away from his ear so that I could hear the conversation. 'Naturally, I want your report Nathaniel, and please speak up because the line seems to be bad.'

'The report is as Your Excellency expected.' English is Leonia's official language, but the Leonese speak it with a jabbering sing-song accent and at times I had difficulty in hearing all that was said. 'Following Your

Excellency's instructions, I first telephoned the Wandsworth Borough Council's housing department and asked them to consult their list of owner-occupiers and leaseholders in the area. As usual you were proved right, Excellency.' Three Excellencies in less than twelve seconds! The caller was a stickler for protocol.

'Though the premises are deemed to be unoccupied, they are still registered in the name of M. Evans and the address is number 309 on the Sussex Coast Road.' The Sussex Coast Road! I raised my eyebrows. The name Evans meant nothing to me, but Mr Brown was a witty little liar. He'd told me that his hide-out was on the Sussex Coast, but neglected to mention that he was referring to a street in South London. It takes a thief to catch a thief and it had taken Hurst-Hutchins, another liar, to rumble him.

'I and my men immediately drove to Wandsworth in two vehicles. A car and a Range-Rover van with the C.D. plates removed, Your Excellency, and we reached the premises at exactly 1700 hours and 52 minutes.'

'You say you have *reached* the premises, Nathaniel?' The bishop broke in angrily. 'Does that mean that they may have seen you?'

'Oh no, have no fear of that, Excellency.' The caller's voice was strident with emphasis. 'The area is in the process of demolition and virtually deserted. Number 309 is one of the few buildings still remaining intact, and we were able to park our vehicles behind a heap of rubble. I am now in a telephone booth about fifty yards down the road and the others are stationed in suitable positions and most unlikely to be spotted.

'As Your Excellency imagined, the place appears to have been some kind of religious establishment and there's a chapel with a clergy house adjoining it.' Hurst-

Hutchins's imagination had either worked overtime or he knew a lot more than he'd told me.

'At first it seemed that both buildings were deserted, but at 1801 hours precisely, signs of life were noted.' The speaker was a stickler for time as well as protocol and I remembered meeting him in Leonia. Mr Nathaniel Swarmi, a wily individual and the bishop's most trusted aide.

'A woman leaned out of one of the ground-floor windows of the house and looked down the road. A young woman with rather a strangely shaped head which appeared skull-like, Excellency.' Too right it did. The woman was either Sally Lambert or Mavis Cato and they were both as bald as coots.

'Hold the line please, because I think something is happening.' Swarmi was excited and he forgot the honorific *Excellency* for once. 'Yes, two taxis have drawn up and one of the drivers has walked to the house and rung the bell. The door has been opened by the short, bearded man you described to me as John Brown and he and a number of other people, including the woman I saw earlier, are walking towards the cabs.

'Ten people altogether. Eight males and two females and with two male exceptions, they are all wearing long top-coats and wide-brimmed hats. They are entering the vehicles ...' There was another pause as Swarmi watched the scene.

'No, not all. The bearded man and another man, who are both bare-headed, are not getting in. As far as I can see they appear to be saying goodbye to their companions, so may I have your orders, Excellency? Shall one of our squads follow the taxis and the rest of us remain on watch here or enter the house?'

'Wait a moment, Nathaniel.' I had jabbed the gun

against Hurst-Hutchins's well-padded ribs and he covered the mouthpiece with his hand, listened to my instructions and delivered them to Swarmi.

'I have no more orders for you, Nathaniel, and there is no need for you to watch the house any longer. Nor must those taxis be followed. Wait till they're out of sight and then go to your vehicles and return here.'

'You really mean that, Excellency?' Mr Swarmi must have been looking forward to the fray and his tone was abject. 'The cabs are leaving now and the two men walking back to the house. I have seven assistants and we are all armed. There is nothing to stop us overpowering the remaining men and following the others as well.'

'I have told you what to do and goodbye, Nathaniel.' Hurst-Hutchins replaced the telephone and grimaced at my revolver. 'You win as usual, Bill. You hold all the aces, everything is going your way and I know your intentions. There are only two people in that house, Braune and another man, and with a pistol you imagine the task should be easy. Truss them up, make Braune tell you where the others have gone, using torture if necessary, and then inform the police.'

He was more or less correct, but though I hoped to give Brown a good hiding, I didn't much care for the word *torture*. It has a medieval ring and a bit of 'roughing up' sounds less sinister.

'But what if you fail, my boy? The odds are two against two; Brown also has a gun and he is a most slippery customer. I hate the thought of you and dear Peggy coming to any harm, so why not take a few of my chaps along and let them do the dirty work?'

'We won't fail.' I spoke with false confidence. Brown was a slippery customer; he and his companion might be hard nuts to crack and for a second I considered accepting the offer. Only for a second, however. If Brown was slippery, Hurst-Hutchins was positively slimy and he'd probably tell one of his half-human gorillas to stick a knife in my back. The bishop was not to be trusted and a set of car keys with a number tag on the desk showed me what action should be taken. I picked the keys up, because the vehicle they belonged to was parked before the french windows which opened on to the drive. A Rover coupé with garish purple paint and an appropriate number-plate, GHH 1.

'The odds will not be two-to-two, because you lied to us Bishop. You tried to restrain us by force and pocket the rewards, and you either knew or guessed where Brown would be hiding. You're going to pay for those lies, and I intend to shorten the odds. Three of us are going to the Sussex Coast Road.' I paused to let the message sink in. Swarmi's vehicles could probably be contacted by two-way radio and if we left him alone Hurst-Hutchins might send them back to the hide-out. When Peggy and I got there our quarries would be handcuffed and on their way to the embassy or Scotland Yard.

'No, Bill, please no. Please tell him that he can't do it, Peggy.' The message had been received loud and clear and the cowardly brute whimpered. 'You can't take me with you. That would be plain murder and leave you conscience-stricken till your dying day. Braune is a maniac whom I exposed to Asmonda for the public good, and I'm sure he's sworn to kill me. If we go to that house I'll be his first target. A helpless target because a priest may not resort to violence even in self-defence.'

'That's your bad luck and you'll be a formidable screen for us, Bishop.' I hadn't thought of that angle and it was a good one. Almost as good as 'for the public good', which was very good indeed. Gerry had betrayed Brown because he thought he was mentally unstable and the betrayal had earned him Asmonda's trust. Mr Brown — or Herr Braune — would have a pleasant surprise when his sought-after victim turned up on the doorstep in full canonicals and he might not notice me till it was too late. If the bishop got shot before I overpowered Brown and his companions, so what? We'd not only have located a nest of dangerous criminals. We'd have saved, or tried to save, the president of a friendly nation. Also, revenge is sweet, and righteous indignation for Gerry's demise would excuse everything. I'd see that Mr Brown was really roughed up before the police were summoned.

'You're being so foolish, Bill, because there's no need for any of us to go to that house.' Hurst-Hutchins's voice was a mixture of squeak and squawk. 'Those people in the taxis are coming here. Hans Braune has sent them to kill me, but forewarned is forearmed and I have a veritable armoury handy and lots of good men.' I was sure that the second statement was true, but the first wasn't. Brown might have it in for the bishop, but he wouldn't risk a full-scale assault on the embassy. He was too downy a bird for that.

'Hans is only the secondary goal, Bill, the rewards are for the others, so all we have to do is wait here and surprise them. Once they're under lock and key, you and dear Peggy can inform the police and I won't claim a penny of the reward money. It'll be yours — all yours.'

If the fat rogue hadn't said that, I might have started

to believe him, but mendacity was clear on his face. Hurst-Hutchins knew that the taxis were not heading for the embassy, and I jabbed him with the gun again and told Peggy to open the windows. Time was running out and, at any moment, Sergeant N'gomo might regain consciousness or be found by one of his fellow thugs.

'Get going, Bishop,' I said, and we took our departure. He, grey-faced and trembling and looking shrunken inside his flowing robes; Peg apprehensive but ready for battle; I with a song in my heart.

Till recently everything had gone wrong for us, but at last the tide seemed to be turning. I felt quite certain that our luck was in and we were about to hit the jackpot.

20

I told Peggy to drive, but when we reached the Rover she said that she'd never handled a car with automatic transmission, so Hurst-Hutchins was made to take the wheel and she climbed into the front seat beside him. I sat in the back so that I could cover him and keep the gun out of sight, though I'd much rather have given it to Peggy and driven myself. But she's always had a misguided soft spot for the bishop and might have become squeamish if the need for disciplinary action arose.

No embassy guards were on hand to interfere with our departure, but the bishop drove badly — bloody badly. It's difficult to make a well-tuned Rover misbehave, but His Lordship managed to. The policeman outside the gates came smartly to the salute as the pennon-bearing bonnet emerged and then leapt back with a curse when the inside front wheel mounted the kerb and bounded towards him. Before we had travelled a mile, four near-misses and one direct hit had been chalked up — the last being a parked bicycle that crashed to earth after contact with our rear wing. Progress was slow and erratic at times; hair-raising at others. Whenever the road was fairly clear, Hurst-Hutchins crawled and wavered. On the bends he accelerated, and if traffic signals were in evidence he attempted to beat the red light and then panicked and jammed on the brakes at the last moment. In a matter of minutes, I felt as pale and shaken as he looked and I told him that if he hoped to attract a police car by his incompetence, he'd better think again. Unless I found Brown and made him talk, I'd spend a long time in chokey or end up before a firing-squad or with a rope around my neck. If ever a man could be described as desperate, I was that man, and an added sentence for murder or grievous bodily harm meant nothing.

'I'm sorry, dear boy. I know I'm not driving well, but I swear it's not deliberate.' He took his eyes off the road while he spoke and we nearly cannoned into a lamp-standard. Like almost every lamp-post I'd seen since leaving the embassy, the thing was festooned with bunting for the ridiculous church conference, and I saw that some of the more observant and unintelligent passers-by raised their hats to Hurst-Hutchins and gave him approving smirks and thumbs-up signs. The idiots probably imagined he was a considerate old buzzard who'd given his chauffeur a rest and was democratically driving himself to Westminster Abbey.

'I'm not used to English regulations and the traffic is so heavy, Bill.' Though he whined with self-pity, the excuses were valid. The bishop had been a long time in Leonia where they drive on the right, and whenever he was out and about in Constitution motor-cycle escorts cleared the way for him.

'I'm also terrified of meeting up with Hans Braune and having a gun pointing at my back doesn't make things easier.' Two more valid excuses, though the gun wasn't actually pointing at his back, but at the back of his seat. An academic distinction, however, because leather and steel springs and whatever motor manufacturers use to pad their vehicles wouldn't stop a high-velocity bullet.

'How did you know that the premises were owned by someone called Evans, Bishop?' I spoke partly for information and partly in the hope that talking might steady his nerves. 'Mr Swarmi used that name.'

'Evans, Bill?' I saw his eyes become furtive in the driving-mirror. 'You must have misheard Nathaniel Swarmi and he is not at his best on a telephone. The only name he mentioned was John Brown. According to you and Peggy that's what Braune now calls himself, so I played a long shot and it happened to come off.'

'Swarmi distinctly said Evans — M. Evans.' I knew he was lying, though I couldn't imagine why when he was completely under my thumb and the whole story would soon be revealed. Maybe from pure perversity. Some people lie because the truth is repellent to their natures and deceit appears a virtue. Hurst-Hutchins was one of those people and if you asked him the time you'd get a false answer. Not an outrageous one which you'd suspect was untrue, of course. Say half an hour either way. Just long enough to make you miss a train or look a fool by turning up too early for a business appointment.

The question was important, though I knew I'd get nothing out of Hurst-Hutchins. John Brown or Hans Braune, a woman in Leonia who had been known as Sarkini Kal or Sissie Mega and a property owner in London called Evans. I somehow sensed that the last name was also the last piece of the puzzle.

'Oh dear me, what is wrong with the damn thing?' A crossing-keeper had raised his STOP sign to let a group of children over and the car shuddered violently to a halt. Even a class car will shudder when the driver has one foot jammed on the brake and the other on the accelerator.

'Nothing's wrong with the car, Bishop, so just concentrate on your driving.' Before the keeper had stepped aside his foot left the brake and we shot forward like a rocket. 'Concentrate, I say.'

'How can I concentrate when I'm probably being taken to my death and there's a pistol behind me? And look at them.' He gave a yelp of indignation and terror. 'Just look at the thoughtless beasts and this car really has gone wrong. I can't steer it or stop it.'

Breakers did lie ahead. A policeman had flagged down the traffic and a troop of life-guards came trotting out of a sidestreet with sabres and breast plates gleaming in the evening sunlight. An impressive spectacle and a formidable hazard, because the car really did appear to have developed mechanical troubles. I could see that Hurst-Hutchins had transferred his foot to the brake and was struggling to turn the wheel, but his labours were in vain. We proceeded straight on towards the lines of horsemen and were almost up to them when I dropped the gun and reached over the bishop's shoulder to give him a hand. The steering felt unnaturally heavy, but our joint efforts saved the life-guards. The car swung sideways, missing one of their steeds by inches and cannoned into a pillar-box. I shot over the seat and landed head first at Peg's feet.

'Are you all right, My Lord? Have you been injured, Mr President?' By the time I'd regained a fairly normal position, help had arrived from several quarters. The officer in command of the troopers had dismounted, pedestrians and motorists were jostling around in the hope of seeing a spectacular blood-bath, and the policeman had wrenched open the driving-seat door.

'Is Your Lordship — Your Excellency — badly hurt?' The rozzer was a snob who must have seen Hurst-

Hutchins's picture in the papers or on the television and he fawned on him without a thought for me or for Peggy, who had slammed her head against the windscreen.

'I'm not sure what damage has been done, but I'm considerably shaken and would be most grateful if you'd lend me a hand, Constable.' The unctuous brute was uninjured, but he managed to look pathetic as he was helped out, and I saw that the collision was not due to mechanical failure. While I was thinking about the property-owning Evans, he had edged the gear-lever from drive to neutral and switched off the ignition. With the engine out of action, the power-assisted steering had ceased to function and a few jabs on the pedal had drained the brake servo-cylinder. The mishap was contrived; Hurst-Hutchins had me by the short hairs and I waited for His Excellency, Lordship or, more appropriately, Lord Shit to spill the beans. The pistol was lying on the car floor and all he had to do was point at it and say he was the victim of a political kidnapping.

I was wrong. Though the whip was in Gerry's hand this time, he didn't seem ready to use it. 'Thank you, Constable,' he said, as he was heaved upright. 'No bones appear to be broken and I'm in fair physical condition, though a bit mentally shaken as might be expected, ladies and gentlemen.' He beamed at the law and the military and the assorted civilians. 'As usual God has spared me for His Service and I can only apologize for my stupidity. An unpardonable lapse of judgment, which might have cost a good man his life, and I have no intention of claiming diplomatic immunity.' The sense of justice impressed his audience and every face showed concern and sympathy. I half expected to hear a ragged rendering of 'For he's a jolly good fellow'.

'Is your station near by, Officer? Ah, only a few hundred yards.' He had taken a couple of steps to see if he was able to walk. 'That is a relief and I would be grateful if I could go there on foot to confess my misdeeds. For some reason, I have developed a sudden aversion towards motor vehicles.' He smiled widely and the onlookers smiled back at him. People like a man who can laugh at his own weaknesses.

'Thank you so much, and there is a further favour I would like to ask of you.' The constable had nodded obsequiously and he looked at the Rover and then at myself and Peggy.

'The vehicle does not seem to be too badly damaged, so I hope you will not need to detain these good people. The gentleman is my chaplain, Father Tonks. A *swinging vicar*, as the young say, who shuns the dog collar, but a true Christian for all that. The lady is his mother and I was about to drop them off on an errand of mercy before going to the Abbey. They have two aged relatives who reside in Westminster and are most anxious to get to them. The poor, dear men are ill. Desperately ill — probably on their deathbeds, and Father Tonks is eager to perform the last rites.' He shut the door and winked at me, but in spite of the onlookers, I felt like climbing out and giving him a punch in the guts. Peggy is a bit older than I, but not all that much older and Mother was a dirty crack.

'Thank you again, Officer. You are a gentleman in the true sense of the word.' The constable had nodded again and started to clear the way for me to reverse from the pillar-box and Hurst-Hutchins smirked through the window.

'All good wishes, my dear Bill. I'm sure you'll need

them, because there's bound to be a death or two during your tussle with Hans Braune.' He drew back and raised his voice so that everybody could hear him.

'Goodbye, Father Tonks, and be in cheerful heart, because the Lord is always with us, in sickness and in health. For Christians death is not a sad end, but a joyous beginning, and if Uncle William or Cousin John die I'll see that they both have really joyous funerals.'

Uncle William and Cousin John ... me and Brown. Hurst-Hutchins probably thought the crack hilarious, but with any luck the last laugh might still be mine. Before making a statement at the police station, the bishop would ask to be allowed to telephone his embassy and he'd talk to Swarmi, who should have returned there by now. But I was a damn sight nearer the goal than Swarmi and already direction signs heralding the Inner London Motorway were looming up. Unless a genuine mechanical breakdown occurred, Peg and I would have concluded our business in the Sussex Coast Road long before Swarmi and his fellow roughs got there.

Uncle William — Cousin John? A feeble joke, but there were other names which were not humorous. Braune or Brown, Sarkini Kal and Sissie Mega and M. Evans. Only the last name meant nothing to me, but I was certain it would complete the puzzle and Peg was helpful for once. 'Ask the *Globe*, darling.' How right she was. A source of knowledge is usually available if you're near a telephone, and I turned off the main road and drew up before a public call-box.

'A chapel in the Sussex Coast Road, Wandsworth, owned by someone called M. Evans who probably has connections with Africa?' The *Daily Globe*'s information service was polite and friendly and ready to oblige as usual.

'Please hold the line while I check with a colleague, sir. We shouldn't be long because she had a similar inquiry not so long ago. From a gentleman at some foreign embassy I understand.' I could guess which embassy and which gentleman had made the inquiry and I waited impatiently for her return.

'Good evening, sir.' Another pleasant female voice came on the line. 'I can give you all the information we have straight away because I made some notes while answering our earlier caller.' There was a slight pause and I heard papers rustle before she started to read aloud. 'The chapel is still registered in the name of Megan Evans, who was born in Llanberis, North Wales, in 1894, and Miss Evans was quite a celebrity for a time. Her parents were devout Catholics and on her fifteenth birthday she was enrolled as a novice in a local nunnery of the Veraline order.

'Have you a pencil handy, sir? There's quite a lot of material to take down?' I hadn't, but I've got a memory like a computer and by the time she'd finished, all the pertinent information was lodged in my brain. I thanked my informant and belted back to the car like a bat out of hell.

'I've got it, Peggy,' I said, as we swung on to a roundabout and headed for the motorway. 'I know everything, or almost everything. I'll tell you what Brown's up to before we reach him, but let me concentrate for a moment.'

I'd done a lot of guesswork about Mr Brown during the last couple of weeks. First, I'd thought he was a misguided do-gooder. Then, I'd swallowed his story about claiming the rewards. Thirdly, I reckoned that he was a sadistic practical joker out for a bit of fun. Finally, I'd half credited Hurst-Hutchins's religious-mania and assassination fears, but also suspected that Brown intended to employ his zombies for more conventional crimes. If Tommy Powell's divine voices ordered him to rob a bank, he'd rob one. If Harry Thorpe was told to produce a batch of nice, used-looking fivers, he'd produce them. If Sally Lambert was instructed to poison some inoffensive old gentleman, she'd poison him. Mr Brown, Braune or Evans had a lot of talents to draw on and the owners of the talents belonged to him. By some strange technique he could control them body, soul and mind, though I hadn't a clue how he did it.

All my early beliefs had been partially correct, but they added up to a total which was far more dramatic than any single one of them taken on its own. Brown's intended crime was not conventional — it was sensational. An operation which had been suggested to him by a dead woman and, in a manner of speaking, Hurst-Hutchins had become his accomplice. That was why the bishop had put us under house arrest after talking to *Canterbury*. Why his secretary had been told to say he was too ill to attend the service *before* we'd got free and threatened him with a gun.

But why had he allowed Peggy and me to make off in the car instead of telling the policeman we were a pair of kidnappers who'd abducted him? I wasn't sure, though I knew that no act of Christian charity was responsible for our freedom. Hurst-Hutchins had had a practical reason for turning us loose and my spirits flagged as the car hummed along the motorway. We were ahead of the field and galloping into the last stretch. But what would be waiting for us at the end of that stretch?

A winning-post, or a whipping-post?

21

Saint — Sinner? Prophet — Impostor? Bride of an angel — Spawn of the Devil? The White Girl — The Old Healer? Megan Evans or Sister Sanctity, which was the title she adopted during her three-year spell in the nunnery, had been called all these things and some of them may well have been correct.

Her stay in the nunnery was unspectacular for two of those years, but the last year bore fruit. Sister Sanctity started to have visions in which Saint Michael visited her in the guise of a bird — a large, brown bird. Not a particularly outrageous delusion, I suppose, but the bird was a fertile fowl and nine months after his first visitation, Sister Sanctity laid an egg. A fine strapping infant who attracted the other nuns' attention by bellowing his head off.

Immaculate conception was Sanctity's excuse, but the Mother Superior wouldn't wear that and she didn't need a papal inquiry to support her scepticism. The Veralines are a nursing order and it was discovered that Sanctity had been romping with a foreign medical student in the linen room of the local hospital.

A serious charge and it changed both their lives. The student was kicked out of college and Sanctity was expelled from her order. Disgraced, dismissed and unfrocked, or whatever they do to nuns; unfrocked sounds a bit kinky.

Her expulsion did not worry Miss Evans. She had

strong faith to support her and an aunt had recently died and left her a bit of money. As the Holy Roman and Apostolic Church no longer required her services, she decided to found a religion of her own and purchased a disused chapel in — Guess where? She and her paramour set up shop and called their creed *Meganism*.

My friendly informant on the *Globe* was a bit hazy about the details of the new religion but I gathered it was a pretty off-beat form of Predestination. If God is all-powerful He must have planned our future careers from the moment of conception and there is nothing we can do to alter His decision. Some of us are automatically selected for paradise. Others, just as automatically, condemned to the old fire and brimstone routine.

Sister Megan, as she now called herself, had her own future well mapped out. She was ordained to spread the gospel all over the earth and die in foreign parts, but her body would be resurrected for a brief period and then brought home. Once in sight of British shores a second miracle would occur. Like Elijah she would be transported to heaven in a chariot of fire and mankind receive the sign to cast off the yoke of orthodox religion. A prophecy which explained the *Pandora*'s end and it seemed that the yoke-casting might be due to follow.

Meganism was a damn silly name to give a gospel, but it attracted quite a following for a while and I could understand why. If one is bound for heaven or hell whatever your conduct, morality is unimportant and you might as well make hay while the sun shines. A lot of people attended the chapel in the Sussex Coast Road, partly from belief and partly because the ex-student, who was a German, had the gift of the gab and could bellow out soul-stirring sermons. But it was he who betrayed her — if doing a bunk counts as betrayal.

Sister Megan's treatment of their son obviously irritated him, because she still clung to the immaculate conception claim and referred to the brat as Michael's Child or Our Redeemer and set out to make him as potty as herself. Germans have a deep love of children. They are also intensely patriotic and both emotions prompted the kraut's departure. The First World War was in the offing and he marched off to do his bit for *das Vaterland*, taking the boy with him.

The loss of her son unhinged Megan even more, and the loss of the amorous preacher emptied her pews. To remedy the second problem, she delivered a sermon stating that all positive actions stem from God and one of her flock took the words to heart. He was convicted of a particularly vicious sexual assault and the authorities gave Sister Megan three choices. Shut up, get out, or be committed to an asylum.

She took the second choice and hooked it to Africa. Europe was decadent and corrupt and at war, but the dark continent contained millions of pure-hearted, simple-minded souls who would be excellent soil for the good seed to flourish in. She was right, though the first crops were nipped in the bud.

Missions were founded in Nigeria and the Gold Coast, but the authorities turned a cold eye on them, and rightly so. Tell a simple-minded man that he can do what he damn well likes and he'll do a lot of very nasty things. Sissie Mega, as the blacks referred to her, was forbidden to preach in any territory under British jurisdiction and Leonia was her next port of call.

'She was the woman Hurst-Hutchins told us about, Bill; Sarkini Kal, the Old Healer.' I'd put Peggy in the picture and as usual her acute mind jumped to the only possible conclusion.

'Of course, and though we've no concrete evidence, I think I can guess who Mr Brown is.' We had left the motorway and I slowed down because, as Swarmi had stated, the neighbourhood was in the process of demolition. The road surface had been scarred and pitted by bulldozer tracks, the street lighting was almost non-existent and piles of rubble loomed through the dusk like bombed ruins. I turned on the headlamps and saw that our goal was in sight. An ugly Victorian chapel with a house beside it and rusty iron railings surrounding both buildings.

'Reach over the back and give me the revolver, Peggy.' I took it from her and slipped it into my pocket together with a box of matches from the glove tray, and I drove past No. 309 Sussex Coast Road, looking for a concealed parking place. Surprise was all-important and I pictured our sudden and unexpected arrival. The door kicked open, the revolver brandished to show my authority and the clipped, self-confident tones of a man who has the upper hand.

'Good evening, Mr Brown, or do you prefer Braune or Evans?' Not that his preferences mattered, because I was in the chair. But it was time that I had a joke at the bastard's expense and I smiled to myself as I switched off the lights and stopped the car behind a pile of broken bricks and debris. Probably the same spot where Swarmi had hidden his vehicles because there was a phone booth nearby. I told Peg to keep close beside me and I stepped out, still smiling because the second part of the act should be most enjoyable. Brown and his companion securely trussed and helpless with papers and furniture and other inflammable materials stacked around them while I produced the match box and delivered the ultimatum.

'This is journey's end, Brown. You tried to burn us alive and you failed. But we won't fail, so listen carefully.' I'd strike a match to show that I meant business and nod at the telephone. There must be a telephone because they had called the taxis from the rank.

'You have exactly two choices. Tell me where the others are and what they intend to do, and then repeat the information to the police after I dial the number and hold the receiver out to you. If you refuse or even hesitate, we shall set this house alight and leave you to fry.'

The scene was so vivid that I could almost hear my own voice speaking, and then I froze. Someone had emerged from the phone-box, something hard had been jammed into the small of my back and another voice spoke. A high-pitched, effeminate and decidedly unpleasant voice.

'Put your hands behind your neck, Easter,' said Sir Jonathan Blake, sadist — psychopath — mass-murderer.

22

'You are rather late.' We had been taken into the house and Mr Brown's surroundings matched his name. He sat before a mahogany table, a russet carpet covered the floor and parchment-shaded lamps glinted on the brown, leather-bound books behind him. Only a television set with its screen aglow, but sound turned down, and the pictures on the walls gave the room colour and variety. The pictures had a single sitter ... a woman painted at various stages of her life.

'Ten minutes late. I was told to expect you on the half-hour. I was also told that you were armed, so please put your weapon on the table and move very slowly.' He nodded at the man stationed by the door. 'Sir Jonathan Blake has a gun and if you do anything foolish he will not kill you cleanly. He will merely cripple you and Mrs Tey by breaking your spines. Sir Jonathan enjoys hurting people.'

'Who tipped you off that we were coming?' I took out the revolver and pushed it towards him. I already knew the answer because there was only one person aware of our intentions. Mr Brown had a partner and the partner's name was Hurst-Hutchins.

'I honestly can't tell you, Bill. I merely received an anonymous phone-call saying that you were on your way here in a Rover coupé and equipped with this.' He balanced the pistol in his hand and, though he was a liar, I believed him. Brown really did not know who his informant was and I began to understand. Hurst-

Hutchins was not a partner, but a manipulator. He wanted the rewards, he wanted Brown's death, and he wasn't going to let Peg or me tell any tales. When Mr Swarmi and his squad arrived, the ensuing battle would produce four corpses.

'I don't blame you for being angry with me, Bill. I did try to burn you on that yacht, but my motives were not cruel or wanton.' I'd heard that line of excuse before when Hurst-Hutchins apologized for locking us up. 'The prophecy had to be fulfilled, you see. A saint — a great priestess — needed companions on her journey to paradise.

'Only that painting was copied from life, I'm afraid.' Brown was staring at a picture of the woman in old age; frail and wizened and leaning on a stick. 'All the others were taken from photographs, newspaper clippings and the imagination. My mother was virtually on her deathbed when we met again.'

'How did you find her?' I didn't really want to know, but it seemed a good idea to keep him talking. Mr Brown intended to murder us, there was little to stop him at the moment, but when Swarmi arrived there might be a chance of escape — a slim one.

'Destiny, Bill. Though Otto Braune, my supposed father, took me to Germany and called me his son, he never mentioned my true parentage. But I always had a sense that I was a vessel ordained to serve God and that feeling grew stronger as the years passed.' His mock jocularity had vanished and he spoke like somebody in the confessional while he told his life story.

A brilliant life. A ship's surgeon with a talent for music and mechanics, who qualified as a sea-going engineer and could probably have made a good living as a concert pianist. After the last world war, the founder of a small electronics firm which blossomed into a gold mine. During that war, a monster: the director of an S.S. research station where experiments in brainwashing were conducted on Jews, Gipsies and others regarded as undesirables by the Nazis.

'A worthless spell on earth, though what I learned in that research establishment stood me in good stead. Shall I show you just how good?' He covered us with the gun, pressed a switch on the hearing-aid receiver which was dangling round his neck and raised it to his lips. Peg and I didn't hear the whispered message but its result horrified us. An electric fire without a guard was glowing near the door and Sir Jonathan Blake stooped and grasped a bar with his left hand. The room reeked of scorching flesh before Brown whispered a second time and Sir Jonathan released his grip and straightened.

'A demonstration of obedience, my dear, but nothing compared to the display you will witness shortly.' Mr Brown looked at his watch and grinned at Peggy's expression.

'All my life the feeling that God was demanding my services persisted, but it was only recently and quite by chance that I realized what He wanted from me.' Sir Jonathan was covering us again and Brown lowered the revolver.

'Yes, destiny brought me to this house, Bill.' Like his brainwashed robots, he spoke with the complete conviction of the insane. 'I sold my business in Germany and decided to travel, and my first call was London. I attended classes at an art school in Chelsea and one day I saw these buildings from the top of a bus. I can't really explain my feelings. They consisted of awe, elation and a sense of homecoming, I suppose, but I left that bus as though a tow-rope was dragging me here. I stood staring at the place for at least an hour and then I started to make inquiries.'

Inquiries which confirmed what fate had in store for him. The premises were still in his mother's name, but they had been empty for years and an estate agent was quite willing to rent them to a well-heeled German. A second-hand book shop supplied an illustrated account of the lady's early career and a photograph of his earthly father standing beside her proved his parentage. He first furnished the house and then set off to Africa to bring Mama home.

'It took me a long time to find her and when I did it was clear that her body could never return to Europe alive.' His eyes swept slowly along the line of pictures. A young girl in a novice's habit; a nun with a set, staring expression which already suggested mania; a middle-aged woman; a crone.

'I painted all those pictures in Leonia, Bill. My personal mementoes of a saint. A martyr who had been derided and reviled and persecuted by ... Them.' The mad eyes glared at the television and I knew that my hunch was correct. The screen showed a floodlit view of Westminster Abbey with police cordons holding back the crowds assembled to see the arrival of the council delegates.

'She was old, Bill. So old and frail in body, but her spirit could not be broken and she knew that Africa was the only place where her gospel could spread. She told me exactly what had to be done and naturally I obeyed.' He looked away from the television set and nodded at one of the paintings. The little waxen girl I'd risked my life to rescue.

'You killed her, didn't you, Brown?' I had no moral

judgment to pass on him and it would have been presumptuous of me to have done so. I'm just an ordinary mortal, while he was semi-divine. A prize-winning colt sired by the Archangel Michael out of Sanctity Sis.

'Naturally, I killed her. What else could I do when that was her wish?' Once again he spoke with absolute assurance. 'So that her word could spread I turned my mother into a waxwork image and gave that image the power of speech.' A slight trace of his old humour returned and he smiled.

'The word did spread. The news of Sarkini Kal's resurrection ran through Leonia like wildfire and my idol was venerated. Soon all Africa would have accepted the faith.

'But one man — one corrupt, evil, lying man ... ' He didn't complete the sentence, and there was no need. I already knew about Hurst-Hutchins's betrayal and I could guess how that betrayal and Sister Sanctity's expulsion from the church would be revenged. The television showed a close-up of the crowd and beneath the hats screening their shaven skulls I saw the faces of Tommy Powell and Bruno Kremer.

'So, it's *Götterdämmerung*, Herr Braune,' I said. 'Because Hurst-Hutchins sold you down the river and your mother was slung out of some one-horse convent in North Wales, you intend to fulfil her prophecy and murder several hundred people — laymen and clergy alike.' Other familiar faces must be in that crowd. Mavis Cato's and the Mackay brothers' and a face I'd once kissed; pretty Sally Lambert's. The gathering made me think of Hassan Sabbah, the Old Man of the Mountains and founder of the *Hashishins*. A crafty character who fed his disciples hemp and told them that the elation caused by the drug was a foretaste of paradise which could be gained by dying in his service. They were then sent out to bump off his enemies and the word *assassin* came into the language.

Clever Mr Brown had copied Sabbah faithfully. All his performing animals, except Sir Jonathan Blake, would be at Westminster and I raised a mental hat to their trainer. Without time-bombs it's difficult to carry out a mass killing. People see the grenades before they're tossed and guns are just as conspicuous. But if the assassins are living bombs with the charges attached to their own bodies and have the will to detonate them, the matter is simpler, and I pictured what might happen when the procession began to move towards the Abbey. A human being would suddenly explode, ripping a path through the police cordon, and the rest of the robots would rush in to join the luckless clerics. Boom — boom — boom! Eight blasts to revenge Sister Sanctity and send Bishop Gerry to another world.

'Very clever, *mein Herr*, though the real prize will escape you.' I have no particular liking for the clergy, but if I could save them I might be able to save myself. Brown wanted Peggy and me to witness his show but he'd kill us afterwards. If the cast was incomplete he might go gaga and make a mistake.

'Hurst-Hutchins won't be attending the service. He realized you were a nut when you met in Africa, and after what we told him today he guessed your intentions. He knows that those people left here in taxis; he approves of what you want to do. That's why he telephoned to warn you we were coming. Why his own men are on the way here now. They won't interfere with your work, but once it's over they'll fix you, Brown.'

'You're a liar, Bill, and a poor one.' Though my statements did not appear to have impressed him he crossed to the television and turned up the volume. 'Why should the man approve of a blood-bath — the slaughter of his colleagues?'

'Because, as you've just said, he is corrupt and evil.' An announcer was describing the arrival of the motorcade outside the Abbey and I raised my voice.

'Hurst-Hutchins has been refused a grant by top members of the church hierarchy and you are about to wipe out a large number of that hierarchy.' I knew that I was speaking the exact truth and I didn't need to make my tone convincing because I'd convinced myself. The Archbishop of Canterbury and the papal legate had rumbled Gerry, and if *Canterbury* and his senior prelates were shipped off to fresh fields and pastures new, there'd be an obvious applicant for the post of primate. Not only a lord bishop, but the president of a nominally Christian country. Gerry's fingers would soon be dipping into the Church Commission's coffers and he'd have all the power he craved.

'I still don't believe you. There'd be an announcement if he wasn't coming.' Brown gestured me to silence with the revolver and stared at the screen. The congregation were leaving their cars and starting to form up for the procession. Robes gleaming in the floodlights, mitres bobbing. An impressive spectacle, but it might end in fiasco because Mr Brown was going into action. He had removed the hearing-aid and connected one of its leads to a wire running up the wall.

'Are you there, children? Can you all hear me, my dear ones?' Though he spoke into the receiver and a hymn was booming from the television, we could make out the words clearly and the voice was not a man's voice any more. The tones were soft and feminine and full of maternal love. Brown was not merely a skilled mimic, he was possessed. Though I'm cynical about the occult, I am quite sure that a dead woman was delivering orders through his lips.

'It is almost time now, children, so be brave and have no fear.' He was looking at the television screen and I saw Sally Lambert. She was receiving the message loud and clear and her face was set in a soulful smile. 'Fulfil your mission at the first stroke of the clock and every sin shall be forgiven. Tonight you will be with me in paradise.' A Biblical reference which suggested that Sister Meg was a forerunner of the more unbalanced Women's Libbers and believed Christ to be female.

'Five minutes to go, Bill, and nothing can stop them. Nothing will stop my angels of death.' Brown had switched off the hearing-aid and his normal voice was resumed. ' "After the saint returns to her place in heaven the mockers will weep." ' I remembered that quotation too. It was one of his Mum's, and Hurst-Hutchins had quoted it to us. 'You and Peggy are mockers, so you must weep with the others, Bill. Weep in hell.'

'The procession is almost complete, but I have just heard that there is one important absentee.' Though I might be very close to death, the announcer's statement raised my hopes. 'The Right Reverend Doctor Gerald Hurst-Hutchins, Bishop of Leonia, has been confined to his bed with gastric flu and is unable to attend the service. Sad news, because Dr Hurst-Hutchins has always been a staunch champion of Christian unity, but I am sure his prayers are with his brother clergy this evening.'

'No — no.' The news might have been sad for some, but it was bloody good for me because Mr Brown's self-control had gone to the winds.

'No — no — no.' His screams drowned the television

and he staggered across the room, stamping the floor like Rumpelstiltskin in a rage. A foolish piece of petulance because he moved between Jonathan Blake and myself and I took advantage of the position. A single, expertly delivered kick sent the revolver spinning from his hand and he reeled sideways, clutching Blake for support.

Blake didn't drop his gun. He had been about to fire it at me, but he was hoist with his own petard. Mr Brown's grasp twisted his hand round and upwards at the exact moment that the trigger clicked home and he crumpled. When he reached the carpet, I saw that part of his head was missing.

'Don't shoot, Peggy, we need him ... we've got to make him stop those people.' She had dived for the revolver and though I shouted at the top of my voice, she failed to see reason. Peg has a mind of her own, a stupid, stubborn mind, and before I could prevent her, she let fly. Brown crashed down beside his henchman, with blood pouring from his forehead. It looked as though the bullet had merely furrowed his brow, but though he wasn't dead, he'd probably be out cold for a while.

'A wonderfully impressive show of faith, ladies and gentlemen.' The announcer's voice was subdued. 'At the head of the gathering you can see His Grace the Archbishop of Canterbury; a truly venerable figure. Beside His Grace is the papal legate, Cardinal Alberti, who must be one of the tallest men present.'

I could certainly see them and they looked like a pillar-box and a telegraph-pole on the move. I could also see Sally Lambert. She was craning over the shoulders of two constables and I knew she was counting the seconds for Big Ben to strike the hour. Sally was Mr Brown's first block-buster. The charge strapped to her body would cut a swathe through the police cordon and allow her companions to dash in for the real killing.

'Don't worry, Bill, I know what to do.' Peggy was bent over Jonathan Blake and she picked up a little plastic capsule that lay beside the torn flesh and splintered bone. 'Mr Brown said they were governed by something called the *Third Ear* and he was speaking the absolute truth.' She handed me the horrid, bloodstained object and I understood. Brown was an electronics expert as well as a doctor of medicine and the capsule contained electronic equipment. The sources of the heavenly voices were tiny radio-receivers which had been planted within the inner ear, and that accounted for damn near everything. The partial deafness and the obedience; how Brown had stopped them killing us after Peggy roughed-up Sally Lambert; why they were prepared to die in his service. Such an obvious ruse — a gimmick which must have appeared in scores of stories and scenarios and I felt ashamed that I hadn't realized the truth earlier.

But there was no time for self-recrimination; no time at all and I hurried to the transmitter: Brown's hearing-aid which was already connected to an aerial for long-range contact. A wail of plainsong was droning from the television and the robed figures were on the march, their purple and scarlet and multi-coloured garments making a nice, bright picture — though here and there were severe tones. Some of the non-conformist ministers wore formal business suits and white shirts, and they resembled magpies among the gayer birds of paradise.

Birds which would be dead ducks unless I called off the hunters and I pressed the switch of the hearing-aid and spoke into its receiver which was really a microphone.

'Now hear this.' An American naval address rasped

from my lips, though I didn't know why. It just seemed appropriate. 'The operation is cancelled — repeat *cancelled*, and all eight of you are to return to base immediately.' My words were commanding, but scarcely feminine or maternal, and I just hoped they would be heeded. Big Ben was about to strike and the hour of reckoning was at hand. I was so intent on delivering the orders and watching the box that I never saw the door burst open.

Mr Nathaniel Swarmi must have heard the shots and imagined we were stopping Brown's blood-bath. He and two other pepper-and-salt characters had entered the room and a brace of machine-pistols were pointing at Peggy and myself. The third pistol was swinging towards Brown who had regained consciousness, and Brown was a tough little cookie. He grasped Blake's automatic and pulled the trigger twice. The first bullet caught Swarmi between the eyes, the second put paid to one of his assistants, but the remaining stalwart ripped Brown apart with a long burst before Peggy winged him and he turned and fled; the gun still going *dudder-dudder-dudder* in his hand.

A real massacre, but my mind was partially fixed on another possible massacre and I heard fragments of the television announcer's commentary between the shots. 'What an inspiring spectacle this is, ladies and gentlemen. A demonstration of Christian fellowship which may solve the Irish problem once and for all. An affirmation of brotherly love that could save humanity from ... '

The voice was cut off by a booming explosion and the set went dead.

POSTSCRIPT

Two Anglican archbishops and seven Catholic cardinals. Two Greek Orthodox patriarchs and a Free Church moderator. Thirty-three fully-fledged bishops and the Unitarian president. Forty-one suffragans and over two hundred smaller fry; archdeacons and deans, provosts and canons and such-like. Mr Brown had planned an impressive slaughter for the history books, but it didn't come off. The boom we heard came from the television's cathode-ray tube, which had been burst by a ricocheting bullet, and nobody around the abbey was hurt. Not even a ruddy curate.

My message did the trick, though not quite as I intended. The shock of hearing a strange voice on the line from heaven was too much for my listeners. They didn't return to base, and if the telly had remained intact we'd have been given the following statement. 'The sight of these assembled clergy marching together in complete harmony has proved too much for some of the spectators. I have just been told that six men and two women have been so emotionally overcome that they are being taken to hospital in a state of collapse.'

Yes, I stopped John Brown's bodies — his Angels of Death, but who'd received the credit? A bastard did, because nobody smashed that bastard's cathode-ray tube, and after listening to the announcement he telephoned Scotland Yard and advised them to search the patients' clothes for explosives and check their fingerprints.

Who got the rewards for the tip-off? The same bastard, though he claimed it in the name of Leonia and stated that his vigilant secret service never believed Bruno Kremer and the others were dead and had been on their trail for some time. The Leonian people didn't get a penny piece of the reward money, naturally. Hurst-Hutchins got it, so what did I get?

A long, rancorous interview with Inspector Dodd who complained that we had withheld information from the police and the Sussex Coast Road massacre need never have occurred. Our statements proved that Peggy and I were the heroes of the hour, but a lot of good they did us. The authorities accepted Hurst-Hutchins's story, as well they might. Gerry had already promised Dodd a bumper, buckshee holiday in Afric's sunny clime. With any luck he may be eaten by a lion.

What were my rewards? Life and liberty, because no charges were preferred against me; £500 compensation for wrongful arrest and a new passport, which I intend to use in the near future.

What have I got apart from the passport and the remains of that £500? For better or worse I've still got a partner. I've got Peg and she's got me. We've got each other, so God bless us both and to hell with Tiny Tim.